COMING~
and~
GOING
MEN

COMING ~
and ~
GOING
MEN

Four Tales by
Paul Fleischman

ILLUSTRATIONS BY
RANDY GAUL

HARPER & ROW, PUBLISHERS

Coming-and-Going Men: Four Tales
Text copyright © 1985 by Paul Fleischman
Illustrations copyright © 1985 by Randy Gaul
Harper & Row Junior Books, 10 East 53rd Street,
New York, N.Y. 10022. Published simultaneously in
Canada by Fitzhenry & Whiteside Limited, Toronto.
Designed by Joyce Hopkins
1 2 3 4 5 6 7 8 9 10
First Edition

Library of Congress Cataloging in Publication Data
Fleischman, Paul.
  Coming-and-going men.

  "A Charlotte Zolotow Book"
  Summary: Four short stories present the adventures of
itinerant artisans and tradesmiths as they travel
through a small town in New England in the year 1800.
  1. Children's stories, American. [1. New England—
Fiction. 2. Short stories] I. Gaul, Randy, ill.
II. Title.
PZ7.F599233Co 1985   [Fic]   84-48336
ISBN 0-06-021883-5
ISBN 0-06-021884-3 (lib. bdg.)

For Dorothy and for Dick

Contents

The
Shade Cutter

I

FRESH SNOW had fallen that morning on the road leading to New Canaan, Vermont. A fresh catalogue of tracks had accumulated since: weasel, wolverine, chipmunk, mink, plus the trail of an apparently three-legged creature whose prints, two very large and one small, stretched miles away to the south. At their head, spruce staff in hand, trudged Mr. Cyrus Snype, cutter of silhouettes.

He descended a hill and surveyed the village: a church, sharp-spired and white as a bride, a graveyard, a green beside it, a gristmill, plus a dozen other buildings clustered about a crossroads.

He halted, huddling within his ancient black coat. No Boston, he thought to himself sourly. Mr. Snype snorted, as was his habit. No Baltimore or Charleston. And yet, he mused, perhaps the very place where *he* might be found.

Propelled by fresh hope, he pushed ahead, crouching forward against the cold. It was January of 1800. A vast sickle of wind swept through the air, mowing down the crop of smoke rising from the chimney tops and attempting to harvest the long-limbed, stalklike figure of Mr. Snype himself.

He scanned the hills dotted with farmhouses, then winced at a powerful stench in the air and found himself passing a tannery, exiled at the edge of the village. He plodded past a blacksmith's, his feet numb due to holes in the soles of both boots. Above him, two crows teetered in the wind, landing on a house whose sign proclaimed its proprietor a buyer of fat and a seller of soap and candles. They cawed as Mr. Snype passed, causing a bald-headed man to dash out the door, snatch up a rock from a pile on his porch, and let fly, sending them flapping away.

"Bad-luck birds," he addressed the silhouette cutter.

Mr. Snype snorted at such superstition, eyed the man's profile, and was not surprised to find his forehead small and sloping, signifying ignorance. He prepared to fling back a scathing reply, informing him that Satan, not crows, was the true source of all misfortune—then, at the last moment, caught himself.

"So they say," he mumbled instead, and marched on, cursing himself at having come so close to speaking his mind to the man. Had he forgotten, he lectured himself, that his own misfortunes had begun just that way? Hadn't he once been renowned as the nation's foremost cutter of silhouettes—as well as their matchless interpreter, a locksmith of the human heart, who could study a shadow and describe, if he dared, the character of the person who cast it? His studios from Savannah to Boston had been filled with patrons of prominence, whose features he'd learned to falsely praise when in fact they'd displayed every variety of vice—which flattery had gained him favor and fame. Until, that is, Satan enticed him into drinking too much at a Charleston ball, causing him to snip the profiles of a lecherous judge and his richly dressed wife in the shapes of a goat and a peacock, respectively. For which acute analysis of his sitters he'd soon found his reputation ruined and his ill fame spread up and down the seaboard, leaving him with no other choice but to give up the great cities in which he was known—and to seek his supper in such spots as New Canaan.

He turned left at the crossroads, passed the schoolhouse, and was pleased to find four of its windows broken. He walked by the cooper's, took note of the heavy padlock on his shed door, and smiled. Signs of corruption had multiplied lately. There could be no doubt that *he*'d been in the area. He felt for the manacles in his pocket, then halted in the middle of the road.

To his right stood New Canaan's only inn. A sign that hung from the porch showed a plow that, swinging back and forth in the wind, appeared to be impatient for spring, turning the plot of air beneath it—and very nearly Mr. Snype's scalp as he climbed the steps and tramped inside.

"Welcome to the Plowshare, sir."

The voice was watchful, canceling its message. Turning, the silhouette cutter beheld sharp-eyed, straight-backed Mrs. Beale suspiciously scrutinizing him through the moving spokes of her spinning wheel. Beside her, two boys looked up from shelling corn into a wooden tub. To her rear, a fire blazed in the hearth, the flames leaping high as though to glimpse the visitor over her shoulder.

"Supper's not for two hours," the woman declared, hoping her guest might leave. Making the house the village tavern and taking in travelers had been her husband's idea. Having come from a long line of ministers, whose stock-in-trade was the depravity of man, she'd acquired a healthy distrust of strangers, which her husband, she often lamented, sadly lacked.

"Bean porridge and beef," stated Mrs. Beale without raising her eyes from her spinning. "Unless it's spoiled," she added suggestively.

Mr. Snype took the hat off his white-haired head and loosened the nooselike scarf around his neck.

"It's thirty cents a night," Mrs. Beale warned.

Mr. Snype set his staff against the wall. He removed

6

from his back the pack that contained his paper and frames, a shirt, some dried beef, plus a black leather book filled with copies of his most eminent sitters' silhouettes, a reminder of his glorious past.

"*Plus* your liquor and tobacco," Mrs. Beale added emphatically. She smiled as if having placed the keystone in an irrefutable argument against staying.

"Agreed."

Mrs. Beale sighed stoically.

"Though most places my room and board come free." Mr. Snype smiled at his hostess through the spokes. "On account of the trade I bring the taproom." He paused to let this enticement take effect, while Mrs. Beale contemplated with dread the prospect of the entire village trooping through the door without knocking—just as if they lived there.

"I cut profiles," Mr. Snype explained, not mentioning his underlying endeavor.

Mrs. Beale eyed his bony face. "Really now. A shade cutter, you say." At least, she thought to herself with relief, he wasn't one of those medicine peddlers, or exhibitors of five-legged dogs.

"I make use of no tracing contraptions whatever," Mr. Snype continued.

Bethany, Mrs. Beale's only daughter, ceased her sweeping and looked in from the taproom.

"I merely view my sitter's shadow and snip, guided by the unaided eye." Mr. Snype clasped his long arms behind him. "An eye, I might add, that's pondered the profiles of the nation's most distinguished figures."

Mrs. Beale wondered if the man was lying. "You're welcome to take off your boots and warm your feet by the fire," she offered, in case he happened to be telling the truth.

Nervously, Mr. Snype cleared his throat. Having painted himself a man of distinction, he thought it wise not to reveal the wretched state of his sole pair of stockings.

"Thank you—just the same," he sputtered.

"Bethany," called out Mrs. Beale, unaware that her daughter's head was in the room. "Come take the gentleman's things upstairs." She glanced at her guest. "You can rest assured your possessions will be safe," she stated, hoping she could say the same for her own.

Briskly, Bethany whisked up Mr. Snype's staff and pack and vanished upstairs, marveling at her mistrustful mother. *Of course* his things would be perfectly safe— why wouldn't they be? She shook her head. In her nearly fifteen years of listening to Rev. Hooke's scorching sermons, amplified all through the week by her mother, she'd never laid eyes on the foul iniquity with which

8

the world was said to be filled. She strode down the hall, reflecting that the only thing in the house that had ever been stolen was her mother's good sleep.

Lifting the latch, she entered the guest room. She set down her load, turned to leave, then glimpsed herself in the mirror and stopped.

There'd be a crowd downstairs tonight, she knew. A profile cutter hadn't passed through in years. She wondered if Oliver Botts might show up, and approached the mirror more closely.

She ran a hand through her lank brown hair. She appraised her nose, inspected her eyes, then carefully composed her lips in a smile. The mirror was missing a chink on one edge, and she gradually moved her reflection that way till she'd ridded herself of the mole on her ear.

She really wasn't so very bad looking, she concluded objectively. Then why had he never noticed her? *Her* eyes were always trained on *him*, loyal as a compass needle to the north. She pursed her lips at this injustice— then noticed the effect this had on her face and quickly reinstated the smile she hoped he might finally notice that night.

She scurried downstairs and dressed to go out to Rev. Hooke's weekly singing class.

9

"You can discuss the price of your keep with my husband," Mrs. Beale was saying as Bethany left. "He's in the barn skinning a cow that died."

"Died?" Mr. Snype's eyes lit up like torches. "Of a sudden, was it? A healthy animal?"

Mrs. Beale glanced up from her spinning. "That's right. This morning it happened. Quick as you blink."

Mr. Snype struggled to hide his excitement. "Yes, of course!" he stammered. "In the barn—we'll discuss it!" He found his way to the back door, stepped outside, and stood, oblivious to the cold.

Animals dying mysteriously. *His* handiwork, and just a few hours old. He could still be in the neighborhood— and might even be lured to the Plowshare that night!

The silhouette cutter trembled. *He*, Satan himself— here in New Canaan! The demon who'd destroyed his entire career that fateful night in Charleston, whom he'd given his life to tracking—and catching.

He produced his iron manacles, both of which were inscribed with the Lord's Prayer. This, he'd learned from a little-known volume, would keep the fiend from changing shape and escaping. And as for detecting him, that would be simple—especially for a cutter of silhouettes. For, in the same book, Mr. Snype had discovered that, though he might take human form, one fact was sure to give him away: the Devil would cast no shadow.

10

II

At the stroke of seven that evening Mr. Snype strode regally into the taproom, to the fanfare of a chiming clock.

A dozen souls had assembled in wait. Travelers were prized in New Canaan: They bore news, a precious commodity. And as the Plowshare was the place where the occasional letter left by the postrider could be claimed, where people came to browse public notices or to enjoy a pipe and a pint of ale, word of the arrival of a rambler—who cut shades besides—had quickly spread.

Mr. Snype placed a low-backed chair near one wall. On a table beside it he set a lamp, then moved the remaining sources of light to the rear of the room and looked over the gathering.

"I see many fine profiles before me," he announced. "Snipping them out's my trade. Who'll be first?" He felt briefly for the manacles in his pocket, then warmed his fingers above the Franklin stove. "My price is fifteen cents apiece, fifty cents framed. Satisfaction guaranteed."

11

Mrs. Pickett, a thick-necked ox of a woman, plowed through the crowd and took possession of the chair.

"What if she *don't happen* to be satisfied?" her husband called out, smiling triumphantly. He was a contentious man, lean as a weasel, whose chief enterprise was suing his neighbors.

"If she's dissatisfied with the shade," Mr. Snype replied, "then there will be no charge." He took up a sheet of black paper while Mr. Pickett grunted and spat some tobacco juice in the general direction of a spittoon.

"Now then," Mr. Snype addressed his sitter, squaring her shoulders and taking note of her curls. He cleared his throat, unbuttoned his coat, and produced a glinting pair of scissors from a leather sheath that hung from his neck. Then he took up a colossuslike stance beside his subject and peered at the wall.

"Excellent," he muttered ironically, irked at finding her shadow on the plaster. He snorted. And a loathsome shadow at that, radiating selfishness.

He opened his scissors and began with her throat. "I've rarely set eyes on a profile denoting such great . . ." He paused. "Such strength of purpose."

Behind him genial Mr. Beale, his face round and red as an apple, grinned without dropping the pipe from his mouth and welcomed more guests, to his wife's irritation.

12

"Strength of purpose?" a voice challenged Mr. Snype. "How'd you come to figure that?"

Mrs. Pickett turned a spiteful eye on the speaker.

"It's inscribed on the chin," Mr. Snype replied, straightening his sitter's head. "And the lips as well. Written out plain." He rounded the bend of her nose with his scissors. "Plain, that is, to one who's studied my system, modeled on the great Lavater's. A system that trains the viewer to comprehend every crease and bump on the brow, every curve of the chin, each—"

"Chins will keep," a man cut him off. He strained forward from his seat like a ship's figurehead, his eyes fixed on the silhouette cutter. "But what about him— being dead. Is it true?"

Mr. Snype looked up from his subject's shadow. "Dead—Lavater? Not that I'm aware—"

"Not *him*. General Washington!"

The silhouette cutter sighed. "I'm afraid so." He returned to his work, his scissors constantly tacking to follow the endless inlets and peninsulas of his sitter's curls. "Struck down back in December, he was."

A gust of disbelief swept through the room.

"When in Boston, I chanced to witness that city's mourning procession," Mr. Snype mused aloud.

The room fell silent, as if the great man's coffin had just been carried past the Plowshare's windows. Faces

13

were solemn, dressed for mourning—except for that of a bent-backed man whose ragged coat bore a British medal and whose birch-white beard hid a smile.

"What's been the weather to the south?" a voice piped up, cautiously lifting the gloom.

Snipping around one final curl, Mr. Snype completed the difficult circumnavigation of Mrs. Pickett's head, a land he hoped never to lay eyes on again.

"Mild," he replied, collecting his payment and seating a toothless old man in the chair. He inhaled the man's barnyard odor, took stock of the rustic crowd around him, and cursed the Devil for casting him out of the perfumed world of the rich and refined.

"Far south, of course, it's been different," he continued. He noted with annoyance his subject's shadow and started in on his Adam's apple. "Charleston hit especially bad, I hear."

The room stirred with sudden interest, while the silhouette cutter ground his teeth at the thought of the site of his ruin.

"Storms the like of which not seen since the Flood." Mr. Snype, who'd lied often in praise of his sitters, knew he was Hell-bound—like the rest of mankind—and blithely added this falsehood to his sins.

"Wharves torn up. Streets flooded. Trees yanked out by the roots like carrots." He grinned vengefully at the thought, confident no one would contradict him. "I re-call hearing that one old oak even came crashing through the roof of a ballroom." Glaring like a wrathful god, he pictured the couple who'd scuttled his career. "Fell right on top of a judge and his wife."

Snipping absently, he contemplated the imagined ruins of the city he'd punished—then felt a twinge of divine mercy.

"The wife survived," he added magnanimously.

His listeners gave thanks for this providence.

"Of course," he continued sternly, "she won't be dancing anymore—being a cripple." Mr. Snype consid-ered his justice and smiled.

"She wouldn't be in that fix if she hadn't been *dancing* to begin with," the deacon's wife spoke up.

Additional proofs of the evils of dancing were heard while Mr. Snype finished the profile, seated a mother and child in the chair—and scowled at the sight of their shadows on the wall.

How long would Satan keep him waiting? he won-dered. There could be no doubt that *he*'d come to New Canaan—every face he'd glimpsed had shown signs of vice. Not that this was unusual. Everywhere he went, *he*'d been there before him, corrupting every corner of the land.

He snorted, speculating on whether any spotless souls

15

inhabited Heaven—or whether, as he suspected, it remained a virgin continent. Picturing the vast, unsettled plains above, he set to work with his scissors just as Bethany charged into the house, an hour late from singing class, and rushed toward the taproom doorway.

She scanned the crowd. Oliver Botts wasn't in it. She brightened at the notion that he still might arrive. And instantly dimmed at the thought that he might already have come and gone.

Still panting, she fetched a bowl of bean porridge. She climbed the stairs, sat down near the top, and hungrily started in on her supper, glancing between the front door and the taproom and fuming at the long-winded Rev. Hooke.

He'd led one last hymn and released the class—then remarked that cultivation of the voice must never displace attention to the text. Which, he'd gone on, in the case of the last hymn, concerned deliverance from evil—which enticed him into an oration on the Devil, a topic that begot further discourses on sinfulness, fire, both common and everlasting, the nature of eternity, plus a tour of Hell.

Bethany pursed her lips to think of possibly missing Oliver for *that.* To listen to Rev. Hooke, she scoffed, you'd suppose that every last soul in New Canaan was black as charcoal and signed over to Satan. She finished

16

her porridge, put down her bowl, and vowed to start worrying about the Devil when she saw him, and not before.

She began licking her spoon, then jumped at the sound of the front door opening and dropped it on the stairs. She reached to grab it. Then she changed her mind and gave it a helping push instead, praying Oliver would pick it up. Skipping downstairs, it clattered to the floor, finally coming to a stop near the giant feet of the Plowshare's latest arrival—portly Mr. Grindstaff, the tanner.

Bethany shuddered at the sight of the man. Eyeing the spoon, Mr. Grindstaff quickly figured its probable weight and worth, glanced about, squatted with a sigh— then caught sight of a girl on the stairs and shot up, disappearing into the taproom.

Bethany paled. He'd intended to steal it! Then again, he might simply have meant to pick it up off the floor— lest someone trip. She marched downstairs, snatched it up, and breathed in the scent of rotting hides that followed Mr. Grindstaff like a ghost. Whatever he'd meant, she loathed the man. Setting her bowl and spoon on a table, she closed her nose to his tannery stink, retreated up the stairs with relief—and stiffened as the front door opened again.

James Botts, joiner and housewright, entered. Behind him appeared his son, Oliver.

Bethany swallowed, her eyes wide as full moons. Wishing she'd left the spoon on the floor, she waited for them to catch sight of her—and watched in dismay as they turned toward the taproom.

Both were tall and both eloquent with mallet and plane and auger and adze, and content to be silent otherwise. Both had sharp eyes, except for those objects that couldn't be chiseled or notched or nailed—including such items as Bethany Beale, who watched them vanish in disbelief.

There—it had happened again! she stormed. He'd left the room, never noticing she was in it! While *she*'d devotedly watched him pass the Plowshare each day on his way to the tannery, where he and his father were making repairs. Watched him pass by morning *and* evening—and never so much as a glance from him!

She trained her eyes on the taproom doorway, couldn't spot him, and chastised herself. She knew every piece of clothing he owned. She'd found out his favorite fishing spots and gone to great pains to discover his birthday. The few words he'd chanced to speak to her she'd memorized like holy scripture—while she, no doubt, appeared only incidentally in his memory if at all, buried in a lengthy entry on a cedar chest he'd helped build for the house, in which she was briefly mentioned as user.

18

She gazed at the chandelier to her right, leaned back, and smiled righteously at the thought of it falling on Oliver's head. Then suddenly she straightened up. Perhaps, if it did, Dr. Coggins would say that it wouldn't be safe to carry him home—and perhaps it would be her duty to nurse him. At last he'd learn the depth of her devotion! She'd change his bandages, feed him, read to him, putting him ever deeper in her debt—until the only equitable repayment would be a proposal of marriage!

She crept downstairs, slipped into the taproom, and stood beside the door.

Mr. Botts was having his profile taken. Oliver was standing beside him. Scanning the room, Bethany searched for catastrophes that might befall him, readying herself to rush to his aid.

Someone might tip over a lamp, she mused. The stove might explode—though she'd never heard of it happening. Tilting her head, she studied the ceiling, ruminating on its sudden collapse. Then she lowered her eyes—and froze at the sight of Oliver, trailing his father, striding toward her.

He paused before her. And then, to her further amazement, opened his mouth to speak.

"I guess that cedar chest's still holding together pretty well," he mumbled.

Bethany wilted. She stared at him, speechless. Seething inside, she managed a nod and watched him disappear out the door.

All he cared about was that plaguey box! Did he ever have a thought that wasn't made of wood?

Dispirited, she sank down in a chair. And to think that she'd been prepared to nurse him night and day—for years if need be!

Smarting from his ingratitude, she decided to sweep him out of her thoughts, like so much dirt, once and for all. Proudly, she set to work, attempting to interest herself in Mr. Snype's craft. She watched his hairy hands at work, noticed his smile while he narrated Charleston's sufferings in further detail, then was called from the room to scrub dishes with her brothers just as Mr. Grindstaff sat for his shade.

"I understand," said the tanner to Mr. Snype, "that you're a master of the shade-cutting trade."

Mr. Snype grimaced at his sitter's stink, glanced at the wall—and saw no shadow. Electrified, he spun around, then realized that the lamp had gone out. Watching glumly as Mr. Beale refilled it, he beheld the tanner's shadow, turned, and could find few faces whose outlines he hadn't snipped. Wearily, he opened his scissors, certain now that he'd missed the Devil. Had he been in New Canaan, he'd have run to the Plowshare and been first to have his profile taken—his vanity would have driven him to it.

"I understand further," Mr. Grindstaff declared, "that you're highly educated on the subject of faces."

Mr. Snype grunted, dejected at the thought that his wanderings weren't over after all.

"And that," Mr. Grindstaff continued, "you can fathom a man with a glance."

The silhouette cutter noted his subject's fleshy chin and jutting lower lip, features he knew to be the hallmarks of greed. "That's right," he replied with a sneer, and snorted.

Mr. Grindstaff cast a glance to his left. He found the crowd thinning, and rested his plump, clasped hands on the beaver hat in his lap. "Then perhaps," he spoke up, lowering his voice, "I could hire your services for a spell."

"I'm afraid not," answered Mr. Snype. "I'll be pegging west to Medford in the morning." Most likely to learn that Satan had headed east, he added sourly to himself.

Mr. Grindstaff eyed the man's boots and was pleased to find the seams parting and the soles worn thin.

"Medford's fifteen miles," he stated. "Those boots will last ten, at the most. Which leaves five."

He smiled at the force of his argument. Mr. Snype stopped cutting and glanced at his feet.

21

"You read faces," said Mr. Grindstaff. "I read leather." He regarded his shadow with admiration. "I am, by occupation, a tanner. A foul-smelling trade, but a profitable one. My spare hides I make into shoes and boots, and I'll send you on your way in a new pair—merely for the brief loan of your eyes."

Mr. Snype led his scissors up his sitter's brow. He didn't need telling that his boots were worn—his feet were still damp from his tramping that day.

"What might you want with my eyes?" he inquired.

Mr. Grindstaff's own pair began to glitter.

"I would have you spy out a particular object." He peered importantly at Mr. Snype. "The rarest in all of Nature. If you can."

"What might that be?" asked the silhouette cutter.

The tanner dropped his voice to a whisper. "An *honest* woman—to be my wife!"

Mr. Snype snorted. A rare object indeed! Among the mighty, whose shades filled his black book, and the meek, among whom he'd sojourned since, he'd not once seen a face, male or female, that expressed incorruptible honesty.

"As a man of some means," Mr. Grindstaff explained, "naturally, the choice of a mate calls for caution."

Completing the tanner's silhouette and finding himself with no further customers, Mr. Snype followed the man

22

to a table and alertly selected a seat upwind.

"The strongbox keys will, of course, stay with me." Mr. Grindstaff fingered a thick chain around his neck. "But since—beyond her other obligations—the woman's duties will include the account book and looking after affairs in my absence, it's essential she have the sum total of my faith. With not a penny's worth withheld."

Mr. Snype smiled to notice the dishonest dimensions of the tanner's nose. Wondering that the man didn't steal from himself, he accepted a complimentary mug of ale from merry-eyed Mr. Beale.

"Naturally," Mr. Grindstaff went on, "I'd prefer a bride with no outstanding debts." He ordered a mixture of cider and rum and, irritated at his neighbor's exemption, paid for his drink with an injured air.

"Someone, preferably, who won't insist on courtship gifts of great expense." The tanner took a sip from his mug. "Ideally, a woman prepared to accept a bull hide ruined by my witless apprentice."

Mr. Snype regarded the tanner with awe. Had he ever, in all his acquaintance with evil, set eyes on a more despicable man? And to think that the knave, whose face shone with deceit, could imagine that an honest woman would have him!

He snorted at the thought and watched the man rise, choose a pipe from the public rack, and fill it with tobacco. With increasing distaste he noted new features, none complimentary, of his puffy face, while the tanner took up the tongs, snatched a coal from the stove, applied it to his pipe, and returned, breathing smoke like a dragon.

"The hills are filled with maidens, mark my word." Mr. Grindstaff sucked deeply on his pipe's long stem. "Take a few days to look them over. Should you find one whose features speak of impeccable honesty, bring me the news." Like a personification of one of the winds, he blew a cloud of smoke across the table. "If she's small and won't cost much in food—all the better."

Mr. Snype swelled with disgust for the man. He imagined the sharp dealing—and out-and-out swindling—he no doubt practiced at the expense of the villagers, who relied on him for their leather. Eyeing the tanner contemptuously, he drank down the last of his ale, snorted—and decided to even the score with the rogue.

"What if I tramp the hills but never set eyes on such a prize?" he asked.

Mr. Grindstaff sipped, loudly, from his mug. "Then I'd be a rattle-capped fool to give you the boots. However, in consideration of your effort, you can lodge with me, at no charge whatever." He performed a few mental calculations. "Excepting, of course, the cost of your meals."

24

Mr. Snype inhaled the scent of fresh hides. "Thank you just the same," he replied. He wondered if there existed a woman who'd willingly walk from the church to the tannery. "I will, however, accept your offer." He curled his lip at the man's stink. "And stay here."

Satan had escaped his grasp as it was, the silhouette cutter reminded himself. And with new boots, he could walk twice as far in a day—and new boots he was determined to wring from the scoundrel.

"Naturally," Mr. Snype continued, "I can't promise you I'll find what you're after." The Devil had seen to that, he reflected. Honesty had vanished from the face of the earth, including, he knew, that portion he occupied. After strolling about New Canaan for a day, he'd tell the man a tale of a face that met honesty's specifications exactly—and take leave of that miserly scamp with a snort and fresh leather under his feet.

"Honesty is indeed a rare item," the tanner stated knowledgeably. He exhaled a dense cloud of smoke. And should Mr. Snype, he mused, actually find a woman possessing it, he himself, lacking the trait, wouldn't scruple at tricking her into appearing dishonest in order to disqualify her—thus thriftily saving the expense of two boots.

"Agreed, then?" Mr. Grindstaff spoke up. Reappearing, moonlike, from behind his cloud, the tanner grinned and extended his hand.

The silhouette cutter, likewise smiling, grasped it and shook it firmly. "Agreed."

Mr. Snype rose late on the following morning. Listening to the wind rub its back on the roof, he'd felt in no rush to set off outdoors—especially on a quest for honesty. Mrs. Beale had been cheered by his absence from breakfast, willing to hope he'd left early, without paying, if only the house might be free of strangers. When he'd finally descended the stairs, staff in hand, she'd glared so fiercely and received the news of his lengthened stay with such offense that he passed up the cornbread, strode out the door, and decided to dine on his hunk of dried beef.

He pulled it from his pocket and wandered up the road. Overhead, gray clouds sped across the sky like broken armies in full retreat, fleeing some debacle beyond the horizon. Sniffing the air for signs of snow, he gnawed on his breakfast and inspected the faces of a trio of girls bound for the schoolhouse.

No sign of honesty there, he scoffed, scarcely surprised at this finding. He snorted. He might as well hope to find fruit on the trees, or the morning sun rising in the west. He pushed ahead, remembering that Diogenes, the ancient Greek, had searched with a lantern for an honest man. And found nothing but moths, Mr. Snype supposed.

He trudged between a pair of farmhouses, using these landmarks to keep track of the road, which was covered, like the rest of the world, with snow. He felt his feet beginning to grow wet and cursed his threadbare, traitorous coat for welcoming in the wind. Shivering, he wished he could dupe Mr. Grindstaff with his tale of an honest woman then and there, but knew that he mustn't seem to have met with such a miracle too quickly.

He greeted a woman with a basket on her arm. Corrupt, he decided. And married besides, to someone less fastidious than the tanner.

He passed in review a row of maples. Chickadees chirped gaily in the branches, causing Mr. Snype to snort at their unceasing, inscrutable cheerfulness. Waving to a man splitting wood, he gazed up at a white house perched on a hill, columned and porticoed like a Greek temple—then noticed that the woodchopper had approached.

"You the shade cutter?" he asked Mr. Snype. His long ears stretched nearly down to his chin, as if he'd leaned too close to a fire and melted.

"That's right."

"I'd like a shade myself. Don't put no faith in money,

though. Not a speck of it. You take country pay?" Not waiting for an answer, the man produced a crushed copper button from his pocket. "It ain't much to look at, until you consider it came from the coat of General Gates—the hero of Saratoga himself. I don't mind saying I was there along with him. Spied it drop off just after the battle. Pounced on it quick as a cat and grabbed it." He grinned and glanced down at the flattened piece of copper. "After his horse stepped on it, of course."

Mr. Snype, eyeing the man's chin, spied deceit, decided he'd never been near Saratoga, then noticed a button missing from his coat, snorted, and continued on his way. All day he tramped the roads around New Canaan, viewing the villagers on whom the tanner preyed. At dusk, cold and wet, he headed for the Plowshare, warmed by the notion of yoking the rogue to an old maid whose features had glowed with guile.

He entered the inn, found supper being served, and was shown to his seat by the cheerful Mr. Beale. Accepting a plate from his wrathful wife, whose hopes that he'd frozen to death had been blasted, Mr. Snype stared in bliss at his bowl of baked beans, raised his eyes—and gaped in amazement.

He felt his heart stop, then start up again. Across the table from him sat Bethany, who'd been late for supper the night before and whom he'd not seen at breakfast, being late himself. For the first time since his arrival in New Canaan, he was able to get a good look at the girl—and discovered, to his spine-straightening wonder, that her face lacked the slightest trace of corruption.

Dumbfounded, he fumbled blindly for his spoon. Could the world contain such a fabled creature, passed over by the Prince of Darkness? In disbelief, he probed her features more closely for any hint of sin. Was she a mirage, and not a miracle? A wisp of smoke, a trick of light? In a trembling voice he asked her for the salt-cellar—and was astounded when she actually set it before him.

Dazed, Mr. Snype started in on his supper, scarcely aware of what he was eating. He scrutinized the girl's eyes and ears, the shape of her chin, the latitude of her cheekbones, searching for the tiniest taint—without success. Committing her features to memory, he put down his spoon, bolted upstairs, and opened his book filled with duplicate silhouettes of his eminent sitters. Dazzled by her virtuous face, he winced at the sight of the sinful before him, reviewed his classification of features—and realized in rapturous wonder that he'd found an honest woman after all.

He stood up, shaky-legged, as if lightning had passed through his limbs, and felt himself a changed man. It

29

was true! he repeated over and over. Finding himself flooded with joy at his discovery of virtue's unsuspected existence, he impulsively promised to reform his own ways, then recalled his bargain with Mr. Grindstaff. Must he hand Bethany, as promised, to such a scoundrel? He winced at the thought—then realized she'd convert even the tanner to honesty and turn him into a model husband, as sure as fire melted ice. Forgetting his planned revenge on the man, he rushed outside to take him the news.

"I do hope he doesn't freeze," Mrs. Beale spoke up, with scant conviction, when he left.

"Weather's warming." Her husband smiled.

Mrs. Beale scowled at the news of this boon. "Wicks need trimming tonight," she told Bethany, wishing she could snip the perennial smile off her husband's face.

Bethany finished her supper and left the table. Fetching the snuffers from the mantelpiece, she began with the candles and lamps in the taproom, trimming off the wicks' charred tips and recalling her talk with Delia Meese. She'd seen her that morning at a quilting bee, and though she'd sworn not to think, much less speak, of Oliver, the subject had drawn her like a dangling thread—and before she knew it she'd unraveled the whole tale.

"So like Letitia in *Passion's Dread Price*," Delia had declared authoritatively. As the daughter of a former peddler of books, much of whose stock was stored in their woodshed, she was privy to a large library on love and recognized as a scholar on the subject. "You've nothing to despair about," she'd promised. "Indifference is merely the stillness before the storm."

Pondering this oracular reply, Bethany, like a bee in a clover field, moved about from wick to wick, eventually making her way upstairs and stepping into the guest room. She tended the lamp beside Mr. Snype's bed, wondering whether, should passion's storm break, she was destined to follow in Letitia's tracks—tracks that led straight to the gates of Hell. Turning about, she headed toward the door—then spotted a book lying open on the floor.

She stooped to examine it. Flipping the pages, she found it was filled with silhouettes—and discovered herself remembering the words of a guest who'd once told her that her shadow was her soul, and warned her never to have her shade cut lest her soul be stolen away.

Bethany stopped at the profile of a child. "Miss Abigail Wilkes, June 10, 1797" was inscribed underneath. Suddenly she shut the book.

Didn't Satan go about collecting souls? And wasn't he said to enter the names of those he'd gained in a book?

She shot to her feet and backed away from the book, recalling Rev. Hooke's words on that very subject the evening before.

The Devil is constantly traveling the earth.

Wasn't Mr. Snype a wanderer as well?

He's known to take joy in raising tempests.

Hadn't she noticed Mr. Snype smile while describing the storms that struck Charleston?

He causes animals to die of a sudden.

Hadn't they just lost a cow, quick as lightning?

Her thoughts aswirl, Bethany assured herself that she must be mistaken. After all, cutting shades didn't make a man Satan, she reminded herself—many practiced that trade. And yet, she answered herself at once, never before had she met with one who kept his silhouettes in a book, or who matched the demon's description so closely.

She edged toward the doorway, not sure what to think. Then the reverend's last words on the subject came to mind, to the effect that the Devil, though he might appear human, could be told by his struggle to hide the one feature he couldn't alter—his cloven feet.

Bethany paled. Staring blankly before her, she thought back to the day before, when Mr. Snype had arrived. She remembered how chilled and wet he'd looked, how her mother had invited him to pull off his boots and warm his feet at the fire. She recalled that he'd looked flustered and *refused*—and knew that the Plowshare's sole guest was in fact none other than Satan himself.

III

The sun, gleaming like a new-minted gold dollar, eased its way into a brilliant blue sky, lighting, in addition to the hills and valleys, the lesser landscape of Mr. Snype's sleeping face.

He opened his eyes, recalled his discovery of the evening before, and smiled. Gazing contentedly out the window, he saw that the sky had been swept clean of clouds, cocked his ear to the merry chirping of the chickadees, found the sound delightful, and emerged from his thick cocoon of blankets—a new man in a new world.

How blind he'd been! he chided himself. He'd been so intent on seeking the Devil that his eyes had been shut to Bethany—that gem of goodness, untainted by *his* touch, whose existence had buoyed him with joy and goodwill.

He approached the window, enchanted by the sight of the snow sparkling in the sun. What a fool he'd been! He'd trained his eyes to search out corruption—and never noticed the beauty that was all around him!

He surveyed the village. It seemed to look fresher, as if it had just sprung into being—and at once he decided that his wanderings were over. He'd arrived in New Canaan and found it true to its name, a land of milk and honey and virtue, and felt no desire to push on farther.

Emptied of interest in pursuing Satan, he removed the manacles from his coat pocket and set them on the table by his bed, sniffed breakfast in the air, and stepped nimbly downstairs.

"Here's your bread and milk," Mrs. Beale beamed, feeling as gay-hearted as her guest. Having found the weather unexpectedly mild, she'd glanced at the almanac that morning and rejoiced to read that deep snows were due, such that the roads might be closed for weeks—and the house mercifully free of travelers.

"There's sausages also. All you can swallow." She handed a bowl to Mr. Snype, who marveled to think that never, until now, had he noticed the woman's sweetness of spirit.

Perhaps his classification of faces had been too harsh, he thought to himself. He'd matched noses and chins

34

with every species of vice—but what of the features that signified virtue?

Sipping his cider, he snorted, heartily scolding himself for maligning mankind. He glanced at Mrs. Beale's cheerful face, knew that people were much better than he'd thought them, and at once began revising his system, reclassifying under "Courage," "Wisdom," "Charity," and other meritorious headings features that had formerly resided among the myriad subclasses of "Sin."

Bethany entered, having finished her chores in the barn, and took a seat far from Mr. Snype. With her face, as he'd seen it the evening before, still glowing in his mind like an afterimage of the sun, he failed to notice the panic in her features, or the fact that she showed no appetite, hurrying off to sweep the taproom.

Mr. Snype smiled in her direction as she left, thinking what a fine wife she'd make the tanner, wishing he were young enough to marry her himself. Looking across the table at her brothers, he noted their own exemplary faces and felt so surrounded by goodness that he vowed to embark at once on his own reform.

He'd begin, he grandly announced to himself, by confessing his criminal scheme to the tanner. Awed by his own saintliness, he gave thanks to Bethany for his renewal—then felt a shiver climb his spine.

What if he'd misread her features? If by some chance

she was filled with deceit, he'd be cheating the unwary Mr. Grindstaff—just when he'd chosen the path of truth.

He listened to the sound of Bethany's broom. Somehow, he had to test the girl.

He rose from the table and entered the taproom. Noting the direction in which she was sweeping, he reached into a pocket, pulled out some coins, and, dropping them purposely on the floor, stooped to pick them up again.

Bethany watched him rise, cross the room, and halt before a window with his back to her. She trembled to think of his true identity—then wondered if she might have been wrong about the man. He *might* be just who he claimed to be, for which reason she'd kept her suspicions to herself.

She struggled to focus her mind on her broom. She'd have to have *proof* before she'd take action—then she spotted a copper cent on the floor.

Her eyebrows jerked upward. It hadn't been there before. Then she glanced at Mr. Snype—and felt her limbs go limp.

He, the Devil, was tempting her—just as Rev. Hooke had said he would! Eyeing the penny, seeing it for the invitation to Hell that it was, Bethany set her jaw, clutched her broom, and proudly swept around it.

Then again, she reasoned with herself, the man *had* dropped some coins on the floor and muttered about

36

his clumsiness. He might easily have missed a penny, she mused—then noticed a silver half dime before her.

She blinked, hoping it was nothing more than a bit of light, and was disappointed. Navigating Satan's shoals, she steered her broom around the coin, cheering herself with the thought that the bright morning light might have blinded Mr. Snype—a line of reasoning abruptly abandoned at the sight of a silver dollar in her path.

Bethany halted, clinging to her broomstick as though to a mast in a hurricane.

"Begging your pardon," she addressed Mr. Snype, struggling to steady her voice. "But I believe you missed a few coins—by mistake." She swallowed, wishing she could believe her words.

Mr. Snype, well pleased with what he'd observed reflected in the window before him, strode toward the money and thanked Bethany. Watching him stoop and snatch it up, she saw that the sole on one boot was coming loose—and made up her mind to give him one last chance to prove himself a mere mortal.

"Being handy with a needle," she began, "I'd be happy to sew up that seam on your boot." She smiled desperately at the man, praying he'd agree to reveal his feet. "It wouldn't be any bother," she pleaded.

Mr. Snype gazed gratefully at the girl. "No need to

trouble your fingers," he answered, thinking of the new boots he'd soon have.

Bethany's heart burst into a gallop.

"Not that your generous offer isn't appreciated," he added. Then he remembered that Mr. Grindstaff had asked to be shown a silhouette of the girl, which Mr. Snype was then to interpret in exhaustive detail before the tanner.

"In return," he spoke up, "allow me to offer my skills in snipping your shade—at no charge."

Bethany glared at the man in terror.

"If you've no objection," Mr. Snype continued, "I'd like to make a copy for myself. To place in my scrapbook, you understand."

Bethany, understanding perfectly, felt her body begin to shake.

"I've my scissors and paper right here," said Mr. Snype, producing them from his coat. "If, by chance, you've a moment to spare."

Bethany stood mute. Shaking her head no, she backed toward the doorway, then whirled about and bolted upstairs to her room.

The silhouette cutter chuckled to himself. The girl was shy. And becomingly modest. Not the sort, like so many others, to leap at the chance to have her shade cut. Convinced beyond doubt of her lofty character, Mr.

Snype retired to his room for a spell, then descended with his staff and set off outdoors.

From her window, Bethany followed his progress. He'd not worn his pack, so he couldn't be leaving. What was he doing? she asked herself, then shivered to realize the answer: Searching for more souls to put in his book.

She contemplated the blue sky and bright snow—and felt nevertheless that the world had grown dark. Satan was walking the earth after all. How could she ever have doubted it? *Of course* Mr. Grindstaff hadn't reached for the spoon that night to keep someone from tripping on it! He'd meant to steal it—as would most of the village if given the same opportunity.

She lay back on her bed, wondering how many familiar faces hid souls black as soot and bound for Hades. She gave thanks that Oliver hadn't had his shade cut— then recalled, horror-struck, that his father had. Instantly she thought back to Rev. Hooke's discourse on the tortures of Hell, then heard her mother approach and enter.

"By the living laws!" She gawked at her daughter. "I told you there's a basket of rye doughnuts waiting to be taken to Reverend Hooke—and here you are lying about in bed."

Bethany sprang to her feet. "I forgot," she stammered, avoiding her mother's eyes. Then suddenly she sought them out.

39

"Did Mr. Snype say where he was headed?" she asked.

"The tannery. To see Mr. Grindstaff, and Mr. Botts' boy, who's working for him."

Bethany stiffened. *"Oliver?"*

"He told me the father was so taken with his shade that he wanted one of his son as well." Mrs. Beale scowled. "But enough. Now be off!"

Her mother left, and Bethany burst into action. Oliver's shade mustn't be cut, she swore, and realized that at last she'd been given the chance to rescue him. Not from fire or collapsing ceilings or falling chandeliers— but from Hell itself!

Madly, she searched for her tallowed shoes, found them beneath the bed, crawled under, and bumped her head sharply crawling out. She slipped them on and rubbed the lump rising from her scalp. She'd *have* to unmask Satan now, she knew. She threw on a shawl, scurried down the hall—then stopped at the open doorway to the guest room. On the table lay a pair of manacles and a key. Darting inside, she snatched them up, thinking she'd better restrain the Devil before revealing his identity and unleashing his wrath.

Flying downstairs, she grabbed the basket of doughnuts, hid the manacles in the bottom, threw open the door, and dashed outside.

She endeavored to run through the shin-deep snow.

The Shade Cutter

Charging down the road, she passed the parsonage. The reverend could wait for his doughnuts, she reasoned. And no doubt he'd approve, in light of her mission. Recalling his words on everlasting fire—that it never went out or needed starting in the morning, and that it fed not on wood but on the souls of the damned—she prayed she'd be able to save Oliver from it, then sighted the tannery up ahead.

She smelled the odor of hides in the air and noticed the stink growing stronger with each step, as if she were approaching Hell itself. Her basket swinging on her arm, she reached Mr. Grindstaff's at last, burst inside, and found the tanner and Mr. Snype at a table.

"And look here!" The silhouette cutter grinned. "The very treasure we've been speaking of!"

Panting, Bethany glanced to her right, saw Oliver and his father repairing a stairway, and rushed up to them.

"Am I too late?"

Father and son eyed her in puzzlement.

"It is indeed too late for you to have *knocked* before entering," Mr. Grindstaff remarked. He tucked a pinch of snuff in his cheek. "I'd expected better manners from a paragon of virtue. Now what do you want?"

"The shade!" she cried, peering at Oliver. "Has he cut it already?"

He pointed proudly to a table. "Have a look."

Bethany felt the blood halt in her veins. Fearfully, she turned toward the table, glimpsed his silhouette, and froze in her pose, her ears ringing with the shrieks of the damned.

"You fancy one yourself?" asked Mr. Botts, returning to prying loose a stair.

Bethany scarcely heard his words.

"No need to inquire," said Mr. Snype. "I've already scissored her splendid profile."

Like a weather vane in a gale, Bethany spun toward the man, her eyes wide with disbelief.

"As you were busy this morning," said the silhouette cutter, "I snipped it from memory—for Mr. Grindstaff here." He held it up for her to see.

Dazed, Bethany stared at her shade, mounted and bordered by a gilded frame.

She'd been caught in his web, she realized trembling— just like Oliver and the rest. There was no use struggling against the fact. She'd mocked her mother and Rev. Hooke, and by the time she'd learned the truth—it was too late.

"Mr. Grindstaff desired that I should interpret your features," Mr. Snype explained. "Before he declared his proposal."

"Proposal?" Bethany exclaimed.

42

Oliver and his father looked up from their work.

"Of marriage, naturally," the tanner spoke up.

The terrors of Hell fled Bethany's brain before this even greater horror.

"Mr. Snype has assured me of your honesty." Mr. Grindstaff raised himself from his chair and strolled around Bethany on a tour of inspection. "Honesty of such a superior grade that he was moved by your features to confess a trespass and pledge himself to a virtuous life."

Mr. Snype smiled. Eyeing the tanner, he realized he'd judged him too harshly at first sight and felt confident now that, as with himself, what petty faults the man might have possessed had flown at the sight of Bethany's face.

"In consequence of which," Mr. Grindstaff continued, "I'm prepared to offer you my hand."

Bethany whitened, then lowered her eyes—and caught hold of the hand the tanner had just mentioned entering the basket that hung from her arm.

"Mr. Grindstaff!"

The tanner's fingers opened, letting fall a gold snuff-box bearing his initials.

"Looked like he was aiming to squirrel it into her basket," Mr. Botts testified.

Mr. Snype's jaw dropped, staggered to find that the

43

rogue remained unreformed after all. "That the girl might appear dishonest," he muttered. "Cheating me out of my new pair of boots!"

Mr. Grindstaff reddened. "Lies!" he cried. "I assure you all that I was merely replacing my snuffbox, so—" He mimed this activity. "And placed, quite by mistake, my hand, so—" He shoved his hand into Bethany's basket, cocked his head, and emerged with the manacles.

Bethany froze.

Mr. Snype bolted forward. "And how did *those* find their way in there?"

The tanner's eyes lit up with alarm. "They're not her lawful property?"

"They're mine!" Mr. Snype spied the Lord's Prayer on each.

Mr. Grindstaff sneered at the silhouette cutter. "Slippery as an eel dipped in lard, aren't you now?" He fixed a knowing eye upon him. "Posing as a man who's put sin behind him—and craftily scheming all the while to pass off a *thief* as an honest woman!"

Befuddled, Mr. Snype turned toward Bethany. "The science of faces," he sputtered, "is, of course, merely in its infancy." Astounded to find his gem a fake, wondering how he'd misjudged the girl, he stared in shock at Bethany—who grabbed the manacles from Mr. Grindstaff.

44

She produced the key and opened them up. "I had a reason for stealing them out of his room!" Though Hell-bound herself, she swelled with her duty to those as naive as she had been—and rushed at the startled silhouette cutter.

"Seize him!" she screamed. Cuffing one wrist, she struggled to grasp Mr. Snype's other hand, while Oliver and his father and Mr. Grindstaff labored to pull her away from the man.

"Fools! Don't you understand?" Thrashing about like a fish on dry land, she ransacked her brain for a way to prove his actual identity to the others, grasped one of his boots, yanked it off—and revealed an uncloven foot.

Bethany gaped. Fighting her attackers, she tugged mightily on his other boot, fell back against a chest of drawers, and saw that that foot was human as well.

"Have you gone hare-headed crazy?" Mr. Snype demanded.

Mortified, Bethany studied the man, amazed to realize that he was nothing more than that. In a daze, she picked herself up off the floor, winced, and rubbed her back where she'd struck it. "Plaguey chest," she muttered absently.

At once, Oliver extended a hand and helped her into a chair.

45

Bethany brightened. Had he noticed her at last? She felt her heart beginning to gain speed. She'd failed to rescue him as she'd planned, yet here he was attending to her—as if he'd been waiting for the same opportunity.

"That's a shame," he mumbled, shaking his head.

Bethany tingled. She looked into his face—and thrilled to find it full of concern.

"Begging your pardon," Oliver continued, "but what exactly is the matter with it?"

Bethany started, as if waking from a dream. "The matter with what?"

"With the chest I built. That you called 'plaguey' just a moment ago."

Bethany's eyes filled with fire.

"The chest?" she stammered. "But I wasn't speaking. . . . Never mind!" she shouted. "It's fine!"

Trembling with anger, she glared at Oliver. So *that* was the source of his grave concern, not *her*! As usual, she reflected. Well then, *let* the ceiling crash down! Let the chimney catch fire and lightning strike him! She'd strut right past him, ignoring his groans. She'd leave him to the crows, she vowed—then she spotted a sliver in one of his fingers. And found herself wishing he'd ask her to remove it.

She turned toward the others. "Please forgive me,"

46

she said. "I'm afraid I've made a dreadful mistake."
She shuddered to think of what she'd done, then noticed
a wave of relief ripple through her.

Her soul *hadn't* been stolen, she realized. Mr. Snype
wasn't Satan—a creature who lived only in her mother's
and Rev. Hooke's dark minds. He'd never corrupted
New Canaan, as they claimed—where people were *good*,
as she'd always known they were.

She handed Mr. Grindstaff his snuffbox, aware now
that the clumsy man had meant to put it in his pocket,
as he'd said.

"As a man of my rarefied tastes," he lamented, "I
expect it's my lot never to find a wife."

"No doubt," muttered Mr. Snype, and snorted. What
a fool he'd been, he castigated himself, to imagine that
honesty walked the earth. Why, he'd as likely meet a
unicorn in the road!

He put on his boots. Taking the key from Bethany,
he unlocked the cuff that encircled one wrist, marveled
at how he'd misread the girl—then noticed something
different about her.

Her profile, he thought to himself. It had changed.

He approached her more closely. It was true—a new
bump! A bump near the crown of the girl's head. A
bump that he'd filed in his original system—which he

now knew had been correct—under the heading of "Thievishness." No wonder the girl had proven dishonest!

He glanced at her silhouette on the table and realized the bump hadn't been there at breakfast. Frantically, he jammed the manacles in his pocket. Nearly bowling over Mr. Grindstaff, he shot across the room and seized his staff.

The girl's corruption, reflected in her features, must have taken place within the hour! While he'd jawed with the tanner, she'd been visited by *him*—who'd already tainted the rest of the village and no doubt continued on his way!

Returning with zeal to his original quest, he dashed outside and up to the inn. He collected his pack. He paid his bill. He ducked under the sign and rushed down the steps.

Mrs. Beale, aglow at the news of his leaving, strode out the door to confirm his departure, watching with relief as he snorted at the chickadees, swore at his boots, set out up the road, and left behind a string of tracks, two large and one small, leading out of New Canaan.

Enemies of
the Eye

"CROWS ARE THE BASEST, most monstrous, depraved creatures that be. Remember that."

Joram looked up from his breakfast. "Yes, sir."

"They devour the farmer's corn."

"Yes, sir."

"They call down the rain and cause floods."

"Yes, sir."

"They bring bad luck to any house they light on. And death if they caw nine times, then fall silent."

Joram gazed uncomfortably at his master. In the week since he'd come from Crawford to New Canaan to serve as Mr. Cobb's apprentice, he'd been instructed frequently on this subject—and wondered each time why he wasn't being lectured on the soap- and candle-making trade instead.

"But that's not the worst, lad. Not by a long chalk."

Joram knew what was coming next and found the chandler's bald head, planetlike, approaching his own from across the table.

"Nay, lad," he whispered hoarsely, point-blank. "The worst of the vile creatures is this: that when they find

51

a bird or beast for their dinner—they always begin with *the eyes*."

Joram nodded gravely. "Yes, sir." Though he'd witnessed crows in this very act, he'd never thought anything of it and was mystified as to why this particular habit burned in his master's thoughts. Was he sworn, as a maker of aids to sight such as candles, to wage war on all enemies of the eye? He himself felt no special dislike for the birds—but, anxious not to displease his new master, strove to seem in agreement. "Most vile, sir."

Mr. Cobb's creased face receded and Joram returned, with relief, to his cornmeal mush. It was spring and the morning was bright with birdsong. The tree out the window was aflutter with finches, and the apprentice was eager to be similarly busy.

"What will our work be today?" he asked. He studied the vast river system of wrinkles emptying into Mr. Cobb's eyes. Then he saw his master's white eyebrows jerk upward—and made out the far-distant cawing of crows.

"Soap," Mr. Cobb answered absently. He spun to his right and peered out the window, his profile matching that of the framed paper silhouette on the wall behind him.

"Hard soap," he murmured. "Plain—not fancy." His

words, as always, were faintly slurred, as though his tongue were a half size too large. Joram regarded his master's gaunt body, straining toward the window like a candle in a draft. Then he noticed that the crows could no longer be heard.

The chandler grunted and faced his apprentice. "Are you blind-eared? I said there's *soap* to be made! Up with you, then, and see to the fire."

Thankfully, Joram jumped to his feet, dashed outside and into the workshop, and set about stacking wood beneath the grate that supported the giant iron kettle. He'd not yet been taught to make soap by Mr. Cobb. He reminded himself to take careful note of all that his master did and said—and imagined his mother watching him proudly. Here he was, the head of the family, applying himself to learning a trade. Something his shiftless father had never done before he'd died that winter—excepting the arts of drinking and swearing. Joram winced at the thought of the man, relieved to reflect that he was turning out tall and lean, unlike his father entirely.

He lit the fire and watched the flames hatch out of the kindling and feed on the logs. In four years' time he'd be a journeyman. And soon after, he hoped, master of his own shop, able to support his mother and sisters. Soap and candles would serve as their herds and fields, faithfully providing for them. And what trade could be more exalted than a chandler's? Light, after all, had been created on the first day. And soap, Joram guessed, hadn't been far behind.

Mr. Cobb entered and opened a keg of lard, which Joram then dumped in the kettle. The apprentice next added a barrel of ox tallow, poured in three buckets of whale oil, then was handed the long applewood stick and instructed to stir—always to the right.

"Never use a stick but of applewood," cautioned the chandler. "And never stir to the left."

Joram inscribed these maxims in his memory.

"Guaranteed to spoil the soap." Mr. Cobb eyed the ceiling suspiciously, then trained his gaze on his apprentice. "And see to it you never let a crow perch on the roof above the kettle and caw."

Earnestly, Joram shook his head. "No, sir." Stirring constantly, he watched Mr. Cobb mix up a bucket of water and lye and lower an egg into it with a spoon. Noting that the egg floated beneath the surface, Joram stirred the liquid into the fat and repeated to himself his master's warning not to let the lye touch his skin or eyes.

"My last apprentice burned a hole in his hand with it." Mr. Cobb scowled, his wrinkles contorting. "The same hand he used to make off with my silver candle-sticks the night he ran off.''

Attentive to the proportions his master used, Joram observed him mix up a stronger solution of lye and water.

"I should have sent the scamp on his way long before,'' the man muttered. "With the toe of my boot.''

Joram watched him lower the egg, saw half the shell now floated above the surface, and vowed to prove to Mr. Cobb that he was no relation to his last apprentice.

"I live upright and expect you to do the same.'' The chandler fished the egg out of the bucket. "You'll find me to be a churchgoing man, who's never missed a service in his life. You'll find me a Sabbath-keeping man as well, and no friend to liquor or cards or foul language.''

Joram stirred with even greater zeal. "Yes, sir,'' he said, and thanked the good fortune that had led him to such an exemplary master—one who knew his craft blindfolded and was a leading citizen of New Canaan besides, having served as selectman and deacon of the church and as captain of the militia as well.

"I've never strayed from my moral in*truc*tion.'' Mr. Cobb had difficulty pronouncing the word. "The in*truc*-tion imparted . . .'' His voice slowed to a stop. His wrinkles wriggled. Joram stared at him and found he appeared dazed, unaware of his surroundings, including the apprentice he'd been addressing.

"Imparted by my mother," he mumbled in wonder, as if this were news he'd never known before. "My mother—by the water, in Georgia. Where we lived. . . ."

Joram cocked his head curiously. He'd thought he'd noticed a slight southern accent to his master's speech, yet the day he'd arrived, Mr. Cobb had chanced to mention that he'd lived in Vermont all his life. Uneasily, he studied the man, who seemed to be struggling to mine more remembrances and was abruptly roused from his reverie by the sound of boots booming into the room.

"Hiding, are you?" their owner spat out. He was a sharp-chinned man, thin as a hayrake. He glared at the chandler. "Aye, with good reason!"

"On the contrary, I'm working," Mr. Cobb replied calmly. "As I've no doubt you ought to be also, Mr. Pickett."

Joram started at hearing the name. He'd never met the man but was already well acquainted with his reputation—as a cross-grained, squabble-seeking idler whose main occupation, to the neglect of his stony farm, was suing his fellow villagers.

"I *am* at my work!" crowed Mr. Pickett. "The never-finished work of defending my rights!" He produced a pair of green candles from a pocket and displayed them with a mocking smile.

"You thought you did me up brown, I expect—passing these off as *bayberry* candles. And tacking two cents apiece to the price!"

Mr. Cobb carefully added the bucket of water and lye to the bubbling fat. "And what other sort of candles might they be?"

"The sort," Mr. Pickett proclaimed, "that don't put out the precious aroma you boasted of. 'Sweet-scented as Paradise,' indeed! They smell a good deal closer to *Hades* to me. At two cents overcharging apiece on a dozen, you owe me twenty-four cents."

Wearily, Mr. Cobb shook his head. He took one of the candles, lit it at the fire, closed his fingers upon the flame, and watched the smoke uncoil through the air. He inhaled deeply. Joram did the same, and smiled at the delicious fragrance.

"You don't smell bayberries?" the chandler asked.

"Not a bit," Mr. Pickett replied. "Now pay up." He grinned hopefully. "Unless you'd care to be sued."

Mr. Cobb studied the man and shrugged. "Reckon your nose just needs a good reaming."

"There's *nothing* needs doing to my nose!" the man snapped. "Why, I can smell a rain coming two weeks before it falls."

The chandler led him up to the kettle. "Then tell me if you can make out the scent of this soap, my finest quality—made from pure hazelnut oil, sweet as nectar."

Mr. Pickett bent over the pot, sniffed, and nodded. "Any fool could smell that."

Joram saw his master's eyes light up. "Then I reckon a fool is what you are—and what the courts would call a man who sniffs *ox tallow* and takes it for nectar. Now be off!"

Dumbfounded, Mr. Pickett gawked at the kettle. Then he leveled a vengeful eye on Joram, as if accusing him of complicity, whirled about, and stormed out the door.

"Worst farmer in the county," Mr. Cobb remarked. He mixed a fresh bucket of water and lye, strong enough to float the egg on its end. "Fences fallen. Seeds late in the ground. And furrows so infernally crooked it would break a snake's back to follow one."

Mr. Cobb examined the contents of the kettle. Then he slowly added the solution of lye and left his apprentice alone to his stirring.

Steadfastly, Joram made use of his stick, ignoring his shoulders' weariness. He reminded himself to stir only to the right. He listened for crows alighting on the roof. Glowing with dedication to his trade, he savored the acrid scent of the soap and marveled that most people found the smell foul. At noon, his master brought him some johnnycake. Inspecting the soap that had risen to the surface, Mr. Cobb skimmed it into a copper pot, tossed in some rosin, brought it to a boil, and the two continued skimming and stirring until the copper pot was nearly full and the soap inside it was smooth as honey.

"Well done," said the chandler when they'd finally finished.

Proudly, Joram hung up his stick.

"We'll let it stand overnight now and cool." Mr. Cobb walked up to a window and found there was still an hour of daylight left. "But tell me now, lad. Can you handle a gun?"

Joram wondered at the question. "Yes, sir."

"Fine," Mr. Cobb murmured with a smile. "Sharp eyes, have you, then?"

"Yes, sir. Middling sharp."

The chandler nodded approvingly. "My own blinkers seem to have lost their edge."

Joram glanced about the room. "Is there any more work to be done?" he piped up.

"No, lad." Mr. Cobb scanned the horizon. "But as the sky's light yet, you've still time to set off with my rifle."

The apprentice was startled by the words.

"And send a few crows down to the Devil."

Joram eyed the man's fringe of white hair, wondering what was transpiring beneath it.

"They're there, mark my words. Thick as fiddlers in Hell. Digging the corn kernels out of the ground, feasting on the beans, bringing on famine. Not to mention murdering newborn lambs." Mr. Cobb faced Joram. "Then jabbing out their eyes."

The apprentice had never heard the birds accused of killing anything so large.

"At town meeting in March the village voted a bounty on crows—ten cents apiece." The chandler trembled at the thought of the creatures, drew close to Joram, and clutched the boy's shoulder. "But sure as sunrise, for each of the blinding birds you bring me, I'll pay you *twelve*."

Bewildered, Joram stared back at the man, unnerved by his inscrutable obsession.

"You'll find the rifle on my bedroom wall. And powder and bullets right beside it."

The apprentice discovered himself strangely loath to take part in Mr. Cobb's war on the crows, even at twelve cents apiece. Then he thought of his mother, knew he ought to jump at the chance to pass on any money to her, and, ever anxious to gain his new master's regard, dutifully walked to the house, fetched the gun, loaded it, and set off.

The sun was getting low. Joram headed east to keep from squinting into the light, winced at the stink of Mr. Grindstaff's tanning pits, passed through a pine grove, and entered a meadow. He glanced about but didn't spot any crows, and found himself wishing he were back in the workshop, mastering the mysteries of candles and soap.

Memorizing his route, he walked on. The snow was melted, mud time had passed, and corn was coming up in the fields. He greeted a man tying gunpowder-sprinkled rags to stakes set among his corn in hopes of frightening the crows away, and another who'd hung up pewter plates whose glinting resembled the flash of rifles. Following a creek, he found berry vines blooming, detoured to the south around a marsh, picked out the sound of blackbirds, then stopped.

Blackbirds, he knew, ate the farmers' corn also—there'd been a bounty on them as well as crows back in Crawford. Why hadn't Mr. Cobb cursed *them*? Not that the man grew any crops himself. But then why should he so despise the crows? Trying to forget the matter, Joram determined to enjoy his ramble, strolled through a meadow, breathed in the sweet scents of grass and earth—then caught sight of it.

It was standing by a birch at the meadow's edge, a hulking crow bent over the ground, intent on eating something. Joram halted, then moved into a crouch. He'd shoot one, he decided, just to please his master, then return to the house before it got dark.

Grasping the gun with his blistered hands, he peered along the barrel and put the crow between the sights. He fired, and was jolted backward by the explosion. Rubbing his shoulder, he bounded ahead, and was surprised to see the bird flapping away above him, cawing mockingly.

Joram stopped. Then he made out a higher-pitched cry behind the calling of the crow. Curiously, he continued on, passed the spot where the bird had been, threaded his way through a maze of brambles—and came upon two black-faced sheep, one of which was bleating shrilly. Sprawled on the ground at its feet lay a lamb.

Joram paled. He rushed up to the lamb, saw blood on its throat, and found it was dead. His bullet must have struck it by accident. He glanced about, noticed a gap in the rock wall running through the undergrowth, and spied a flock of sheep on the other side. Wishing the mother would stop her bleating, he drove the pair back into their field, then glimpsed a sign nailed to a tree. Approaching, Joram parted its veil of vines and found it a warning to trespassers to keep to the side of the wall they were on—at the risk of being sued by Mr. Roderick Pickett.

Mr. Pickett! The apprentice gaped at the name. The same man Mr. Cobb had made a fool of that morning—and who was no doubt spoiling for a chance at revenge. Fearfully, Joram recalled the spiteful glance the rogue had shot him. He'd be happy as a hungry weasel in a henhouse when he found out what had happened. He'd sue Joram on every charge he could think of. And likely Mr. Cobb as well, as the owner of the gun and legal guardian of the bullet. Since he earned no wage as a mere apprentice, any payment, Joram realized, would have to come out of his master's pocket—and suddenly it occurred to him that Mr. Cobb might even dismiss him outright. He'd not signed a contract or paid any fee. The chandler could shuck him at a moment's notice. And hadn't the man wished aloud that he'd done just that with his last apprentice?

Joram stiffened. Then he made up his mind. He would tell no one about the lamb.

Mr. Pickett, after all, had broken the law by letting

his sheep roam his neighbor's land. Had he bothered to keep his walls in repair, the accident would never have happened.

Quickly, Joram looked about him. There didn't seem to have been any witnesses, and Mr. Pickett's house was nowhere in sight. Being the careless farmer he was, he'd most likely never notice the loss of the animal—if he'd ever noticed its presence in the first place.

He returned to the lamb and gazed down upon it. He'd nothing to worry about, he told himself. A crow might have killed it, for all anyone knew. Hadn't Mr. Cobb declared that they did? He waited a few minutes for one to drop down and stab out its eyes, but none appeared. Using a fallen branch for a shovel he dug a hole, buried the lamb, masked the grave with twigs and leaves, and hurried home through the dusk.

He approached his master's house.

"Any crows?"

Joram started, then realized Mr. Cobb must be sitting on the porch in the darkness.

"No, sir," he stammered in reply. "None at all."

The creaking of a rocking chair reached Joram's ears. "Clever-headed birds, they are. Don't lose heart." The rocking stopped. "Before your apprenticeship's through, I guarantee you'll have shot the eye-eaters by the score."

Joram brightened to hear his continuation with the chandler spoken of so surely.

"I warrant you'll send a few to Old Splitfoot tomorrow," Mr. Cobb comforted him.

Joram swelled with the desire to impress his master. "Yes, sir," he vowed. "I shall."

In the morning Joram reheated the soap, stirred in salt, allowed it to cool, then ladled it into a mold to harden, and was once more dispatched by Mr. Cobb to hunt crows.

The apprentice went eagerly this time, as he did throughout the two weeks that followed, stalking the birds with a desperate zeal and slaying them in ever greater numbers.

He studied their flight, their habits, their calls, tramping till he could scarcely see his gun sights, cursing the daily coming of night. His anxiousness over Mr. Pickett's lamb filled him with boundless energy and a seething animosity toward his prey. He ceased puzzling over his master's motives and came to agree with his assessment of the birds. Each one he brought down seemed fresh confirmation that they were villainous creatures who deserved to be shot—and must therefore be guilty of hideous crimes. Among them the killing of newborn lambs,

which outrage in particular he felt himself to be aveng-
ing, wondering as he walked home one evening whether
or not a crow, and not he, had in fact felled Mr. Pickett's
animal.

"Fine, lad!" his master greeted him at the door. He
opened Joram's sack, found eight crows inside, and gaily
counted into the boy's palm his payment for the afternoon's harvest. "You'll grow rich at this rate, and drive
the despicable birds clear out of Vermont altogether!"

Joram grinned, oblivious of the coins but keenly aware
of Mr. Cobb's approval. He sat down and cleaned the
man's gun with great care, proud that the chandler
trusted him with it, glad to be distinguished from his
thieving predecessor.

"I used to shoot the blinding birds myself," his master
reminisced. "By the bushelful—with that very rifle."

Raptly, Joram oiled the stock.

"It was given to me . . ." The chandler's voice trailed
off. He seemed lost in a dream, his eyes frozen in place.
"On my thirteenth birthday—by my father," he announced, as if he were amazed to learn this fact.

Joram stared at his master with concern. The man,
he knew, was in one of his dazes that came on when
his memories bubbled to the surface.

"At the two-story house, with the view of the harbor. . . ."

66

Blinking, Mr. Cobb emerged from his spell, and at once reached for his Bible. "I've never forgotten my moral in*truc*tion," he affirmed to his puzzled apprentice. He took a seat, delivered his nightly reading, then retired.

The next day Joram dipped two hundred candles and listened to his master's detailed account of his part in the battle of Bennington, marveling that his memory was suddenly so sharp and wondering whether his slightly thick speech was the result of an injury from the war. In the afternoon Joram was released to shoot crows. He fetched the rifle, struck out up the road, and noticed a crowd in front of the Plowshare.

The apprentice approached. In the center he found a barrel-bellied man shaking hands all around, who he learned was Mr. Hamby, a seller of ballads and broadsides whose yearly arrival was as regular as the robins' and as welcome, and considered by many the only sure sign of spring.

Walking up to his horse, the man opened a saddlebag and returned with a sheaf of papers.

"As I promised," he declared, "a fine crop of new verses to divert the old and instruct the young—all for a mere five cents apiece." He pulled out a sheet. "'A lamentation on the sudden decease of James Starr,' for instance." He scanned the gathering with his squinty eyes. "Who drowned in the mighty waters off Cape Ann."

Joram observed the crowd stir with interest. Smiling, Mr. Hamby drew out another.

" 'A sprinkling of tears on the dust of Reverend Poole of Plainfield,' " he bellowed like a town crier. He looked up. "Not to mention a half-dozen elegies, most affecting, on our glorious General Washington, who put on immortality this past winter."

Shuffling his sheets, Mr. Hamby continued to tempt his audience with the titles of versified tales of shipwreck, accounts of tornados, meditations on the meaning of earthquakes, marching songs, hunting ballads, and commentaries on politics. He delivered the first lines of a poem concerning God's wrath as expressed by a fire in Boston, and declined the offer of a long-eared man who proposed to buy it with a crushed copper button that he claimed had fallen from the coat of Ethan Allen at the taking of Fort Ticonderoga. Mr. Hamby then read from a piece on the smallpox, followed by a stanza from a lament of two lovers, causing, Joram noticed, Bethany Beale to nod sympathetically and sigh.

"As for crimes," Mr. Hamby announced with relish, "that is to say, warnings to the young to avoid evil, what better example than that of Nat Greer, hanged not long back just southward in Sheffield." Without looking at the page, he began to recite. " 'A dreadful tale prepare to hear, of the shameless miller, Nathaniel Greer. . . .' "

Joram turned and made his way through the crowd.

"I've also 'An apprentice's dying groans, exhorting the young to be cautious of small crimes.' "

Joram froze.

"The instructive account of a lad who first lied to his master, progressed to stealing, and finally killed the old man and ran off." Mr. Hamby smiled pleasantly. "And was devoured by a pack of wild dogs."

Wide-eyed, Joram hurried away, half expecting Mr. Hamby to order him to halt, shouting out his secret to the world.

He veered across the village green, glad to be out of the gathering's sight. Was he following the wicked apprentice's path? he wondered to himself. Would his one misdeed beget another, leading him inevitably toward the gallows? He strode through a cornfield, then passed a dead crow hanging from a pole as a warning to others, spat at the bird, and knew he'd nothing to fear. *He*'d committed no crime—a crow had killed the lamb. The one he'd shot at had been standing watch. He'd missed it, but at least he'd kept the killer from feasting on its victim's eyes.

Filled with revulsion for the birds, he marched on,

mercilessly hunting them down, taking pride in ridding the earth of the wretches. Crossing a field, he stooped to put his sixth crow in his sack and was approached by a man.

"Well, now. A local Orion on my land."

Joram looked up. The man towered above him, his sleek beaver hat and deep eyes appearing impossibly distant from his shining black boots.

"Beg pardon, sir?"

The man viewed him with scorn. "Orion," he stated wearily, "was a mighty hunter in the myths of the Greeks." He sneered at the sight of Joram's rifle. "Whose weapon, I might add, was a club, not a gun. And whose prey was considerably fiercer than crows."

Joram stood up and glanced curiously at the columned white house to his right. "They eat corn," he spoke up in his defense. "And kill lambs."

"Lambs! Truly now!" The man laughed in derision. "Is there no crime that can't be blamed on the crows?" Contemptuously, he peered at the apprentice. "Perhaps, though I doubt it, it would interest you to know that the ancients *revered* crows and ravens."

Joram was taken aback by this claim.

"Prized, they were, for their powers of prophecy and their skill at learning human speech. Would you believe me if I told you that the birds in your bag were honored as symbols of hope and long life? That Apollo chose the crow as his messenger—the bird that sees all, and knows all as well?''

Uneasily, Joram laid his eyes on the sack at his feet. ''Yes, sir,'' he replied.

''In your Bible the birds are esteemed as well, as the righteous instruments of justice.''

The apprentice thought hard, able only to recall the crow that Noah released from the ark.

'' 'The eye that mocks the father,' '' the man quoted, '' 'and scorns to obey a mother will be picked out by the ravens of the valley . . .' ''

Petrified, Joram remembered the line—and fearfully scanned the field for crows.

''Proverbs,'' added the man. ''Chapter thirty.''

At once, Joram snatched up his sack and hurried off, his brief sympathy for crows vanished.

Hadn't his mother told him that Mr. Cobb was to be obeyed like a father? And if, by chance, his bullet *had* struck the lamb, hadn't he broken his master's commandment to live upright by not telling Mr. Pickett about it? He climbed over a fence and recalled that the evil apprentice Mr. Hamby had mentioned had been punished for his crimes by wild dogs—and felt suddenly sure that the crows of New Canaan intended to carry out upon him the sentence named in the Bible: blindness.

71

He spied a crow on a fence post, fired, and missed, sending it flapping out of sight. Frantically, he sought others to shoot, seeing each crow as his knowing accuser, hearing his guilt proclaimed in their caws, shivering at the sight of their heavy beaks.

At dusk he returned, uncheered by his master's delight at his bulging sack of birds. That night he dreamed a crow told Mr. Pickett, in perfect English, of his shooting the lamb, at which point the man donned a judge's wig and demanded Joram be sent back to his mother. He awoke in a sweat, Mr. Pickett's cackle ringing in his ears—and abruptly sat up.

The man neglected his farm, it was true—but that didn't ensure he'd never notice the lamb's loss. On the contrary, Joram realized, he was just the sort to count his sheep now and then *in hopes* of finding one missing, giving him cause to sue someone about it.

Terror-stricken, the apprentice lay back. Then suddenly he had an idea. He'd stop Mr. Pickett before he got started, by shooting a crow, taking it to him, and telling him one of his lambs was dead—killed by the crow, which he'd shot just before it plucked out its victim's eyes. If Mr. Pickett asked to see the lamb, he'd claim that he'd buried it, to keep off more crows. And should he ask Joram to lead him to the grave, he'd lead him about and claim he couldn't find it again, since the lamb that he'd buried wouldn't look freshly dead.

His mind miles away from cutting wicks and melting tallow, Joram spent the day rehearsing what he'd say, and was at last released with his master's rifle.

He set off through a field, saw a crow, and shot it. Picking it up by the legs, he walked on and reached the road that led past Mr. Pickett's just as Mr. Hamby, reciting one of his verses aloud, passed by on his horse.

"Well, now!" the man interrupted himself. He smiled at Joram and walked his horse alongside him. "Come to see me out of town, have you, lad?"

The apprentice was feeling distinctly unsociable but felt he couldn't simply bolt ahead down the road.

Mr. Hamby leaned down toward Joram and winked. "Or might you be strolling to your fair lady love's?"

"No, sir," Joram stated firmly.

Mr. Hamby chuckled. "Well, then, since it's *me* you were thinking about all along, it's the least I can do to declaim you a verse—free of charge—to keep us both company. What manner of piece do you fancy hearing?"

Joram faced straight ahead down the road, as if Mr. Hamby weren't there at all, and cursed Mr. Pickett for living a full mile and a half farther on. "Don't care," he replied, striding along briskly.

"Don't care?" The broadside seller appeared stung by this show of indifference to his wares. "Well, now, what would you say to the tale of the most fearsome monster of a man that ever walked up Ladder Lane and down Hemp Street?"

Puzzled, Joram glanced at Mr. Hamby.

"That ever took ill with rope fever," the man added. "And the double throat distemper, besides."

"Beg pardon?"

Mr. Hamby sighed. "That was ever *hanged* for his abominable crimes—and not fifty miles off, in Sheffield, at that." Pleased to find he had the boy's full attention, he cleared his throat and threw back his head.

" 'A dreadful tale prepare to hear, of the shameless miller, Nathaniel Greer. . . .' "

Joram recalled hearing the words the day before and found himself listening with interest as Mr. Hamby recited, by heart, twelve stanzas describing Nat Greer's grisly murder of his sweetheart, the refrain to each being his strange claim, "I remember not any such miscreant act."

Mr. Hamby concluded and turned toward Joram. "I don't mind saying that you've heard my most popular verse, you have. A trump—yes, indeed." He smiled with satisfaction at the thought. "It's many a meal old Nat Greer's bought me, and many a bed he's put under

74

my bones. Without him cutting out his dear Dora's heart, I don't doubt that my own would have stopped before now."

Joram glanced up at the broadside seller. "And it happened just to the south—in Sheffield?"

"Printed on the page, for all to see." Mr. Hamby lowered his voice a notch. "Though just between us, in truth it happened elsewhere, but turned out so amazing popular that one of my Boston printers brings out a fresh edition every few years—dressing it up to his fancy, changing names and putting it somewhere new on the map."

Joram felt a sudden loss of interest in the tale.

"Not that it's any less beneficial to the morals of the young," Mr. Hamby spoke up. "But if I'm not mistaken, the actual crime happened back before the war. And wasn't truly a murder."

Joram spied Mr. Pickett's house far off. Wishing his companion would stop chattering, he quickly repeated his lines in his head.

"No, he never laid hands on her heart," Mr. Hamby mused. "It was her eyes he went for."

The apprentice interrupted his speech to Mr. Pickett and looked at the broadside seller.

"Just like your crow, there. Blinded the girl, for making eyes at another man."

Joram cocked his head. "Blinded her?"

"Aye, lad, that's right." Mr. Hamby grinned, taking obvious pleasure in the gruesome tale. "Blinded her with lye—he being a soapmaker."

Joram stopped dead in his tracks.

"A soapmaker? Are you certain of it?"

Mr. Hamby brought his horse to a halt. "Sure as there's wool on the back of a sheep. He lived down south, along the coast. Savannah, I believe it was."

Dumbstruck, Joram recalled Mr. Cobb retrieving from his memory his having lived in Georgia—in a house with a view of a harbor. And yet, he realized, laughing at himself, the chandler clearly hadn't been hanged.

The two continued down the road.

"Claimed to be an honest, upright citizen," Mr. Hamby rambled on.

"What was his name?" the apprentice inquired.

Mr. Hamby smiled at this display of interest. "The knave's real name I don't remember, and I reckon there's few enough who do. If he'd gone to the gallows, it might—"

"Then he *wasn't* hanged?" Joram interrupted. He halted. Mr. Hamby stopped beside him.

"Nay, lad. He wasn't a murderer, like my precious

76

Nat Greer, bless his evil soul. The scamp, I recall, suffered only a hole bored in his tongue with a hot awl—and was booted out of Savannah, I don't doubt."

Stone-faced, Joram stared at Mr. Hamby—and remembered his master's slurred speech.

"Said all the while he was a man of high morals. With no recollection of the crime at all."

Joram thought of Mr. Cobb's dazes. No wonder he knew nothing of his distant past! The crime had been too shocking to accept as the work of his own virtuous hands, and must have been purged, with the rest of his life in Georgia, from his memory—intruding only during his spells.

Joram lowered his eyes toward his crow and felt a sudden wave of sickness at the thought of the dozens of its kind he'd killed. Mr. Cobb couldn't admit to being a blinder, so he'd cursed the crows in his place—just as Joram himself had done. At once, the apprentice dropped the bird and, leaving Mr. Hamby gazing on him in wonder, spun around and headed back to Mr. Cobb's.

He broke into a run, his own problems forgotten. He reminded himself that Mr. Hamby had never mentioned Mr. Cobb—and couldn't recall the blinder's real name—and wondered whether he was wrong about his master. Approaching the house, he spotted the chandler rush out, grab a rock from the pile on the porch, and dash into the road, looking up at his roof.

"Thought I heard a crow," he addressed the apprentice.

Joram scanned the roof but saw no birds.

"There, just beside the chimney. I'm certain . . ." His cocked arm gradually relaxed.

Joram caught his breath and cleared his throat.

"I've a question."

"Yes," the man muttered in reply, still searching for the phantom crow.

"Did you practice your trade in the state of Georgia?" The apprentice struggled to steady his voice. "In the town of Savannah—before the war?"

Mr. Cobb gave a start. His wrinkles writhed and his eyes seemed to lose their focus on the roof.

"Georgia?" The chandler repeated the word as if he'd never heard it before. "I've always lived here. In Vermont—in New Canaan." His voice was weak, as though he were mumbling in his sleep.

Joram gathered up his courage. "Did you ever commit a crime?" he stammered. He studied his master's blank gaze. "A blinding?"

Mr. Cobb's eyes widened. His wrinkles twitched.

"I've never forgotten my moral in*truct*ion! I'm a churchgoing man, incapable of such a monstrous, depraved deed as that!"

"Then you *didn't* blind your sweetheart with lye from your shop?" Joram asked desperately. "For looking at another?"

He peered at his master expectantly, waiting for the old man's lips to move. When they did, Joram realized he'd heard the words before.

"I remember not any such miscreant act."

That evening Joram walked to Mr. Pickett's and told him he'd shot one of his lambs by accident. He saw the man's eyes light up, listened to his greedy demand for payment—failing which he'd be forced to sue Joram and his master—then watched his face fall upon being presented with the sum of Joram's crow-killing money, exceeding even the amount he'd asked for.

On returning, Joram found that Mr. Cobb had gone to bed. Staring at the candle left burning in the window, he felt suddenly drained of all desire to make a life from tallow and wax—and lye. Hoping his mother might have heard of another master in need of an apprentice, he tied up his belongings in his winter coat, headed toward the door, then stopped.

He stepped over to a barrel. He lifted off the lid and dug out a handful of shelled corn. Then he walked out the door and down the steps. And tossed the kernels on the ground for the crows.

Slaves of
Sham

I

MR. SIMEON FYFE—sign painter, frame gilder, mirror silverer, varnisher, portraitist, as well as exhibitor of panoramas, most recently of the life of Washington—guided his horse and cart around a pothole, and suddenly pointed his hand at a tree trunk.

"Color of that shadow on the bark!" he called out.

Patrick, his son and assistant, perched beside him, spun to his right and stared. "Brown!" he shot back.

"And what shade of brown?"

"Sienna. With a bit of blue mixed in."

The limner smiled and plucked out a handkerchief. "Fine, lad. Always see the world as it is." He blotted his face, round as a pallet and shining with sweat in place of paint. "Unlike *the others*, who'd have said it was black—the color they suppose all shadows to be."

Patrick sneered at the thought of them: their gawking, gullible customers, who were unable to see things for what they were, who gaped at their portraits as if at a living creature instead of paint daubed on canvas, who took pride in the satin they were shown to be wearing despite the fact they owned nothing but homespun. And who were likewise enthralled by the heroic exploits of

Washington, even though, Patrick knew, they were no more real than the man's painted picture.

"Behold the straight-up-and-down truth at all times. Let that be your motto, Patrick my lad." Mr. Fyfe swatted a deerfly orbiting his head and winced at a pain in his shoulder. "Never succumb to sham like the rest!"

Patrick noticed him rubbing his arm.

"Pesky bullet," mumbled Mr. Fyfe, eyeing the shoulder of his radish-red coat. The following day would be the Fourth of July, and he cringed at the prospect of prayers and speeches and toasts in honor of Washington—the man he'd so worshiped during the war that he'd run off at fourteen, Patrick's age now, and volunteered to fight. And had promptly been led by that thimble-witted general to defeat by the British at Germantown, where Mr. Fyfe, heading for home at a run, had acquired a musket ball in his shoulder.

"And beware of heroes!" the limner warned his son. He snarled at the thought of Washington, the fool who'd spent most of the war in retreat, then been handed the victory at Yorktown by the even more addlebrained British. "Beware!"

Patrick nodded and narrowed his eyes—eyes he'd trained to pierce all pretense.

"Behind the hero's myth stands a man, lad. Puny, pockmarked, eyes dim, teeth gone." Mr. Fyfe scowled,

84

his stout body tightening. "A shameless scoundrel, more often than not, and most likely doomed to smell brimstone through a nail hole when he dies."

Patrick glimpsed a church spire in the distance and reflected on the irony of their serving as Washington's apostles, spreading his legend throughout the land. But what choice had they had? Their mare had gone lame, marooning them in Salem, where work was scarce and their funds soon ran low. Then Washington died, men wept in the streets—and they quickly converted their panorama from "Scenes in the Procession of History from Eden to the Present Day" to "Prospects of the Glorious Life and Deeds of General Washington," which title they'd painted on the sides of their cart, and had drawn such crowds that they were on their way west, behind a fresh horse, in four days' time.

Mr. Fyfe angled his eyes toward Patrick. "A body, of course, has to eat," he spoke up, musing, like his son, on their mode of survival.

"Yes, sir," agreed Patrick, well aware that they'd not missed a meal since leaving Salem.

"And though our hero-hungry audiences, enslaved by sham, are duped, *we* aren't. Not for the hind end of an instant."

"No, sir," Patrick replied. He lowered his hat against the afternoon sun and spied a girl strolling toward them down the road, reading from a book while she walked. She looked up as they approached, fair-haired as Patrick himself and approximately his age, smiling and waving her hand when they passed.

"But above all," Mr. Fyfe exhorted, "gird yourself against the most beguiling of all illusions—*love*."

Patrick nodded attentively.

"It's nothing but a species of deceit, like painting. The entrancing image of the beloved—a mirage, not on canvas but in the mind."

The limner glanced at a woman hoeing weeds and thought back, bitterly, to his wife. "I took your mother for a goddess when I met her. An angel from heaven walking the earth." He grimaced to think of the faithless shrew, who, the first time he'd taken Patrick with him on his travels, had taken the opportunity to run off with another man. "The most pernicious of all delusions— which you, forewarned, will, I trust, resist."

Patrick adopted his most skeptical squint, daring the female world to deceive him. Peering ahead, he sighted a shack, on the porch of which he beheld no beckoning maidens but, rather, a white-bearded man sitting on a stool and whittling amidst an archipelago of sleeping dogs. The man stared up the road at the cart, made out the advertisement on its side, spat, and proudly polished a British medal pinned to his shirt.

"Washington!" he muttered acidly to his dogs, the loyal band that followed him everywhere, a canine version of the army he dreamed of one day leading in the cause of returning America to King George. "Praise *God* he's gone to the worms, I say."

"And good day to you, sir," Mr. Fyfe piped up as they passed, mistaking the man's words for a greeting. Amiably, Patrick lifted his hat and made use of the chance to wipe the sweat from his brow. To his left, a band of swallows skimmed over a field of rye, catching his eye and leading it toward the village ahead.

"What's this we're coming into?" he asked.

His father slapped a mosquito. "New Canaan." They passed a gristmill and rounded a bend. "Reckon we'll stop here and put a show on tomorrow."

They reached the crossroads and clattered past the school, causing the windows to fill with faces, then halted in the shade of a row of great patriarchal maples at the edge of the green.

"You tend to Bess." Mr. Fyfe climbed down and gave their horse a pat on the rump. "I'll see about scaring up bed and board." He set off and Patrick jumped to the ground. He placed the jacks under the cart shafts, unhitched Bess, turned her loose on the green, and sat back against one of the maple trees. Overhead, cicadas droned in the branches. A thrush's song, made miniature by distance, carried to his ears. Drowsily, he watched the horse graze.

"You part of this here?"

Patrick shot to his feet. Startled, he whirled about and found a long-eared man standing nearby.

"Yes, sir," he replied.

The man eyed the cart, fanning himself with a limp black hat. " 'Prospects of the glorious life . . .' " He turned toward Patrick. "What manner of prospects?"

"Painted—on a panorama. Fifty yards long, passing right before your eyes, every scene as real as life. We'll be showing it to the public tomorrow."

The man returned his hat to his head. "Washington," he murmured reverently. "Greatest general the sun's shone on since Caesar."

A sour smile crept out of the corners of Patrick's mouth.

"What's the charge for the show?"

"Ten cents," replied Patrick.

The man stepped closer and reached into a pocket. "Fair enough. Though myself, I don't put no trust in money. Never have." He produced a battered copper button, displaying it to Patrick on his palm. "But I'm sure you'll agree this button here's worth the price of the show—and a deal more. Especially when you consider it came from the coat of General Montgomery himself."

The man beamed at Patrick, expecting the boy's eyes to light up, but found his face blank.

"Montgomery, the martyred hero!" he bellowed. "Who laid down his life at the battle of Quebec!"

Patrick sneered contemptuously, feeling safe in assuming General Montgomery was as unworthy of the term "hero" as the other rogues who wore it.

"We don't want his precious button," he stated.

The man gaped at him in disbelief. "*Don't want* the button of one of America's greatest military men?"

"We don't put much stock in heroes," declared Patrick. He imagined his father looking on proudly. "American or any other kind."

The man's eyebrows flew up. He sprang back from Patrick as if realizing he'd been speaking with Satan.

"Imagine it—such talk from a stripling! And tomorrow Independence Day!" He polished the button and put it safely in his pocket. "No more patriotism than a pinch bug!"

He marched down the road, then stopped and turned. "Your kind should be prosecuted! For treason!"

Patrick watched him storm away, sighing at the man's

submission to sham. A few minutes later his father returned.

"Fetch Bess and lead her over yonder." He pointed to a house just across the road. "They'll feed her, and us, and give us a bed. In trade for painting a scene in the parlor."

Patrick ambled after the horse while Mr. Fyfe climbed into the cart. Raising the panorama's heavy rollers, he set them on their feet a yard apart, cranked past a stretch of unpainted canvas, and stopped when Washington's portrait appeared. Then he lowered his stubby legs to the ground, and set off with his tin chest of painting supplies, allowing, as he often did, the departed President to gaze out upon the green world of the living as an added advertisement.

"Now then, Mrs. Meese." Mr. Fyfe set down his chest in the parlor and faced his patron, a thin woman beating a bowl of bread dough while she looked at the wall above the mantel. "What will you have?"

"Something with the sea," Mrs. Meese answered absently. "I saw it once, as a child. At Portsmouth." She turned. "If it's not too difficult, that is."

"Too difficult? Tush!" The limner swelled. "Why, we'll paint you a sea so thundering real that you'll feel the spray in your face when you pass! You'll hear sea gulls squawk and taste salt in the air—and have to plug your ears with wool at night to keep out the crashing of the waves!"

Mrs. Meese, assuring herself he was joking, retreated from the room just as Patrick entered.

"A sea scene," Mr. Fyfe spoke up.

Patrick nodded, threw open the tin chest, and briskly unpacked pallet and charcoal, rags, stencils, squirrel-hair brushes, paints, and the rest of the tools of illusion.

"We'll need Prussian blue," Mr. Fyfe announced.

Patrick opened a leather pouch and poured a blue powder into his mortar. Then he added several drops of flax oil, picked up his pestle, and commenced to grind just as the Meeses' front door opened.

Delia, Mrs. Meese's only daughter, entered the house and halted at once. A grating noise reached her ears. Approaching the parlor, she glanced inside—and was startled by the sight of the pair she'd passed earlier.

"I expect we'll need more vermilion as well," Mr. Fyfe went on, his back to the doorway.

Awed, Delia watched the man sketching a ship in charcoal on the whitewashed wood. Looking to her left, she saw Patrick's eyes rise and spot her, note the book in her hand, and seem to light with recognition. The sound of his grinding suddenly ceased.

"And more black, of course," Mr. Fyfe continued.

Patrick recalled his father's warning and furiously returned to his work, watched in wonder by Delia—who thought back at once to Arabel Wilde.

Hadn't the heroine of *Runaway Heart* met her love when he'd knocked at her door, seeking work? Arabel's visitor, however, was a tinker, while hers was an *artist*, attuned, like herself, to the sublime—the kindred spirit she'd craved.

"Delia?"

Her mother called her to her chores—chores she contrived to carry out as close to the parlor as possible. She dusted the room with uncommon thoroughness, watching Patrick load his father's palette. She swept the floor, eyeing his fine features. She trimmed the lamp wicks, noting his smooth hands. She sat carding wool just outside the door, hoarding every word the painters spoke.

"That red fine enough?" Patrick's voice inquired.

"Well ground," replied his father's. "Smooth as butter."

Delia rested her hands in her lap. Why couldn't her family converse on such things? Or anyone else in New Canaan for that matter? She plucked a fresh tuft of wool from her basket and combed it out, knowing the answer. Their minds were on crops and cows, not art. Beauty to them was a full root cellar and a barn stuffed to the rafters with hay. How coarse they all must appear to the limners—they who cultivated their sensibilities rather than bean fields, who weren't tethered to farms but roamed the land, who'd perhaps seen London and Paris and Rome, feasting on the world's beauties, feeding not simply their stomachs but their souls.

She glanced at Patrick, wondering if he'd any inkling that she was different from the rest, then thought back again to Arabel Wilde. Her tinker, she recalled, had stayed just an hour but had found himself unable to forget her, returning years later to reveal himself a count and carry her away to his estate. Patrick and his father, Delia's mother had mentioned, would be leaving the following afternoon. She must make the most of her opportunity.

"Delia!" Her mother called her to the kitchen. Her father and her four brothers, all older, trooped in from the fields, a human herd made restless by the smell of supper. Before it could be served, however, Mr. Fyfe invited the family to the parlor to behold the wall above the mantel, now adorned with a ship riding out a storm, bordered by diamonds stenciled in red.

Mrs. Meese gawked at the ferocious waves, not present in her memory of the sea's serenity. "It's not quite," she stammered, "as I recall. At Portsmouth."

Her husband grunted. Her sons shuffled their feet.

"Though I'm sure it's quite lifelike." Mrs. Meese forced a smile.

"I don't doubt you'll find sand on the floor," Mr. Fyfe spoke up with a grin. "Left by the tides."

Mrs. Meese eyed the painting suspiciously, picturing seaweed draped over her chairs.

"Well, *I* find it splendid," Delia declared.

All heads turned her way. Fearlessly, she put forth her position that the scene showed feeling, that the boiling sea could be seen as a fitting metaphor for the passion-racked heart, that while others might shun strong emotion, she, like the painting's creators, did not.

Her parents appeared astonished by this outburst. Her brothers looked baffled. What else could she expect? Proudly, she turned her eyes toward Patrick—and was startled to find him as dismayed as the rest, then realized he was no doubt merely stunned to discover a defender of art in New Canaan.

"Smoked eels for supper," Mrs. Meese broke the silence.

She left the parlor, trailed by the others. The meal was served, during which Mr. Meese told of his life as a traveling bookseller, his spotting the future Mrs. Meese from the road, his yanking the reins, and his bringing

94

his wagon of books to a permanent halt in New Canaan—
a tale of love that repelled Mr. Fyfe and caused Delia,
while clearing the table, to frown at the thought that
the object of his passion had ever since been his cornfield.

She scrubbed the dishes, put them away, and was visited by Bethany Beale. With her father's books at her
fingertips, among them a shelf of romantic novels, Delia
was held to be an expert on love. After listening to
her friend's latest disappointment in her endless pursuit
of Oliver Botts, she led her to the books, which were
stored in the woodshed, opened, with scholarly respect,
a small volume, and read aloud the passage she'd sought,
consoling her client with the far greater trials faced by
Rosanna in *River of Tears*.

It was dark when Delia saw Bethany out. Patrick
glanced up at the girls when they passed, then returned
to helping his father gild a frame containing a silhouette
of Mrs. Meese. When, shortly after, they'd finished, Mrs.
Meese presented them, as promised, with a bottle of
her black cherry brandy in payment. Taking this and
their tin chest to the cart, Patrick spied storm clouds
moving toward the moon, knew the panorama ought
to come down, hoisted himself up, turned the crank—
and froze at the sound of the fabric tearing.

He studied the canvas in the moonlight, and suddenly felt his skin turn chill. Leaping to the ground, he dashed toward the Meeses', and feverishly returned with his father.

"Someone took a knife and made cuts, right here!" he burst out, pointing. "Top to bottom. They left a few threads to hold it together, then cranked it back a bit to hide it."

Staggered, Mr. Fyfe climbed into the cart. "So that when we started the show," he thought aloud, gingerly turning the crank and watching the rip extend another foot, "the panorama—would tear in two."

Patrick, whose duties included crouching behind the canvas, hidden from view, and invisibly cranking the fabric forward, shuddered at this possibility.

"So that we," Mr. Fyfe went on, "should seem fools."

He scowled at the rip and surveyed the village. "Any notion what clevershins might be behind it?"

At once, Patrick recalled the man with the button, whom he'd sent stalking off in a rage. Guiltily, he blurted out the tale of the man's offer and his unwise reply.

"Montgomery's button!" his father swore. "I'd likely have told the scamp off same as you."

Together they lowered the panorama, slipped it into its leather sheath, hopped to the ground, and headed back toward the Meeses', failing to notice the prints left by a pack of dogs who'd trailed their master to and from the cart that evening.

"No harm done," Mr. Fyfe crowed confidently. "We'll sew up the rip in the morning." He smiled. "And settle with that button-peddling scoundrel as well."

II

The sun rose into a cloudless sky on the morning of July Fourth, conferring shadows on all things upstanding, among them two horses plodding toward New Canaan, the wagon they were drawing along the road, and Mr. Isaiah Clapshaw, sitting straight-backed on the seat, clutching the reins.

The wagon jolted suddenly. "Pothole," Mr. Clapshaw spoke out.

He was tall and grim-jawed, and so bony he seemed to have been picked over by a flock of vultures. On his head he wore a tattered top hat, which brushed against a branch and brought down upon him a second-hand fall of rain.

"Bit of shower in the night," he announced.

A pair of sheep viewed the passing wagon. Its high wooden sides had been fitted with windows and supported a peaked, shingled roof. In this house on wheels Mr. Clapshaw had slept beside the road, pushing on at first light.

He peered ahead and sighted a steeple. "Village coming up," he called out. His horses lifted their ears at the words, though this message, like the others, was meant not for them but for the passenger enclosed in the back.

To his left, Mr. Clapshaw eyed a weed-choked cornfield. He passed a sign threatening trespassers, then spied a herd of cows who'd escaped their pasture and were blocking the road ahead. Instantly, he grabbed for his whip.

"Lift your legs, you miserable loafers!"

He halted at the edge of the herd and lashed at the air with all his strength.

"Have you any idea who's waiting to pass?" He glared at the cows, furious with their incomprehension. "Insolent beasts!"

As if stung by this insult, the herd slowly parted. Importantly, Mr. Clapshaw shook the reins.

"I'll thank you to show more respect next time!" he

snapped, speaking not on behalf of his own injured honor but that of his passenger, the illustrious figure who'd accompanied him on his wanderings for thirteen years—during which time, while Mr. Clapshaw's hair had gradually turned to gray, then white, no sign of aging had altered his consort. Which was scarcely surprising, since he wasn't a creature of flesh but of wax, modeled and dressed to resemble George Washington.

"Cows," the exhibitor explained to his companion.

He continued on, passing signs warning off sheep stealers, fruit pickers, and fence hoppers in general. All of a sudden, from his right, a horse and shay commanded by Mrs. Pickett came clattering down the path from her house and into the road just in front of him. Both parties pulled sharply on their reins.

"Madam!" Mr. Clapshaw barked. "Kindly turn your horse aside at once and allow us to proceed on our way."

Mrs. Pickett, a stocky woman straining the seams of a calico dress she'd just finished, studied the stranger's odd wagon and snorted. "You reckon you own the roads, like royalty?"

Mr. Clapshaw, his patience drained by the cows, shot to his feet. "Perhaps," he burst out, "you'd care to know

99

that *General Washington* rides in my wagon—and wishes to pass!"

"Truly, now." The woman smiled. "Stepped out of the bone orchard for a spell, has he?"

"A waxwork!" the exhibitor roared. Though for the past six months he'd indulged more freely in the fancy that he escorted the real Washington—a notion no longer contradicted by the existence of his model's original, a man Mr. Clapshaw had at times regarded as nothing other than a dangerous imposter.

"Carved," he added, "by my own two hands. Viewed by uncountable multitudes."

"Do tell," Mrs. Pickett replied, unimpressed.

"Including, this day, the residents of the village ahead. Now move aside!"

Mrs. Pickett was in no particular rush to hear Rev. Hooke's Independence Day blessing. Or to check the Plowshare for any waiting letters. Or to take in the day's festivities, which Mr. Pickett was missing in favor of putting in writing his side of his latest court suit. This, however, failed to outweigh the fact that her gray mare's white front feet stood in front of those of Mr. Clapshaw's team. Which allowed her to suddenly snap her reins, speed off down the road in front of the man, and enshroud him with the dust of her departure in reply to his insufferable arrogance.

100

Fuming, Mr. Clapshaw strangled the reins. He ground his teeth, waiting for the dust to settle, and finally pushed on.

"Small disagreement," he reported, straining to keep his voice under control.

He struggled to forget the affront, brushed the dust off his coat, and felt the sun on his neck. Steam was rising from the wagon's damp roof. The day was already heating up. Much like *that* day, he thought to himself. The day that Washington, reviewing his troops, had paused to praise Mr. Clapshaw on his depiction, carved into the stock of his rifle, of the robed female figure "Liberty" vanquishing the serpent "Tyranny." Which brief contact had blazed in his memory with the brilliance of a sun ever since, the fact at the center of a gradually enlarged myth of his intimacy with the great man.

"Corn waist-high," he spoke out.

A pair of swifts swooped over the wagon. Ahead, Mr. Clapshaw sighted a shack—and jerked to his feet in disbelief. The porch was littered with dozing dogs, whose owner, determined to hear not the slightest sound of the holiday celebrations, had shuttered the windows and bolted the door, sealing himself within his four walls—from one of which hung a British flag.

Aghast, Mr. Clapshaw averted his eyes and hurried his passenger past the outrage. "Rye looking healthy," he piped up quickly, shielding him from the fact of the flag.

He passed a gristmill, entered New Canaan, rumbled alongside the green—then stopped. Before him stood the Fyfes' cart. In wonder, he read the advertisement on its side, taken aback to discover another roving disciple of Washington in the village. Proceeding to the opposite side of the green, he drew to a halt and took note of the crowd squeezing into the meetinghouse. Nimbly, Mr. Clapshaw stepped down, threw open the door at the rear of the wagon, climbed inside, and readied the room: untying the ropes that bound the seated Washington to his chair and the chair to the wagon, adjusting his wig, smoothing his white breeches, spreading the map on the table beside him. He blew the dust from his boots and black coat. Then he neatened the bed on which he himself slept, surveyed the scene, felt satisfied that it was ready to be viewed that afternoon, climbed back out, and entered the church.

Rev. Hooke mounted the pulpit and, when all were seated, gave the holiday blessing. Bowed heads were lifted, then quickly lowered again as the reverend, inspired by the occasion, launched without pause into an anecdote concerning his part in the taking of Trenton, followed by a strategic analysis of the battle, a description of the clothing and customs of the Hessians, and a history of the use of mercenaries worldwide. When he'd finished, those of his listeners who were still able to raise their heads joined in a hymn. Mr. Critch, the deacon, then rose, produced a broadside purchased that spring from Mr. Hamby, and proceeded to recite an elegy on the death of General Washington—a reading that drew tears from the congregation's eyes, to the hearty disgust of Mr. Fyfe and Patrick. Another hymn was then sung and a speech delivered. Delia Meese then stood and declaimed a poem she'd composed on the love of country—which love she compared to that between a man and a woman in its passion and permanence—attempting, while she spoke, to catch Patrick's eye. A last hymn was then sung, following which Rev. Hooke released his flock with the thought that although the day was one of leisure, Satan would no doubt be laboring furiously, an observation that brought forth a series of knowing nods from Mrs. Beale.

The crowd rose. A band of boys raced up the back stairs and commenced to ring the bell. The villagers made their way toward the green, trailed by the limners, who climbed into their cart, sewed up the rips in the panorama, and set it on its feet, ready to be shown.

"No sign of the slyboots who sliced it?" asked Mr. Fyfe.

Patrick shook his head. "Maybe he stayed home."

The limner asked his son to describe him, then hopped to the ground. On the green, Mr. Diggs, the blacksmith, was standing beside a cannon, delivering a speech in praise of republican government. Mr. Fyfe approached, stopping beside a bald-headed man at the edge of the crowd.

"Beg pardon," said the limner.

Mr. Cobb turned and faced him.

"I'm a stranger hereabouts. Looking to find a lanky man that wears a black felt hat."

The chandler eyed Mr. Fyfe in puzzlement.

"The scamp pulled a rascally trick—or tried to," the limner explained. "Took offense to my boy. Told the lad he ought to be hauled to court—for *treason.* All on account—"

"Roderick Pickett. Sure as crows in the corn." Mr. Cobb's stomach soured at the thought of the man. "He'd sue the sun itself for not shining on a cloudy day, if he could find a way." He turned. "Haven't seen him about. But that's his horse and shay, over yonder." He pointed through a stand of trees toward the Plowshare.

Mr. Fyfe smiled. "Much obliged," he replied.

He walked to the inn and glanced around. No one seemed to be about. Pretending to admire the Picketts' gray mare, he stroked her mane, then opened his knife, quickly cut through all but a hair of the straps that bound her to the shafts of the shay, and innocently returned to his cart.

"Reckon we're even with the rogue," he said, hoisting himself up. "Slice for slice."

His son stared at him curiously.

"He'll reap his own knavery when he sets off for home." Mr. Fyfe grinned. "I guarantee it."

Patrick smiled and studied the strange-looking wagon parked across the green. Suddenly the crowd broke into applause and Mr. Diggs led a toast to "our glorious union." Firecrackers erupted nearby. Another speech was given and another toast joined, this time to "the Day," followed by salutes to "the President," "the sovereign state of Vermont," "Ethan Allen," and "the soldiers of 'seventy-six." The Declaration of Independence was then read, and the cannon, loaded with rags, fired off, causing the horses to rear in fright.

The crowd dispersed about the green. Sensing that the moment was right, Mr. Fyfe nudged his son and pointed to his bugle, which Patrick snatched up and blew mightily.

"Gents and ladies—your attention!" the limner shouted, standing up in the cart.

Patrick pushed another breath through the bugle.

"The panorama—the wonder of the age—is ready to pass before your awed eyes! Showing scenes from the life and exploits of our valiant General Washington."

The crowd began to wander his way, gathering about the side of the cart on which the panorama was stationed.

"At a charge," Mr. Fyfe continued, stepping to the ground, "of a mere ten cents apiece."

Patrick circulated about, his hat held out, collecting the coins. Then he climbed up into the cart and, hidden from view behind the panorama, strapped on a small drum, rummaged for his sticks, and quickly executed a roll.

"Washington!" boomed Mr. Fyfe. Standing in front of the crowd, he turned and glanced up at his subject's determined features. "The infant who would make mighty England tremble was born on his father's Virginia plantation."

Hurriedly, Patrick sat down on a stool and turned the crank at the base of the roller, bringing a landscape of great lushness into view.

"Here he learned farming and the art of surveying." Mr. Fyfe faced the painting, recalled their haste to produce a panorama on Washington's life, and smiled to consider how much time they'd saved by using the backgrounds from their scenes of world history—in this case, their rendition of the Garden of Eden, in the foreground of which they'd added a house.

"As a lad, he surveyed in the Shenandoah Valley.

While still a young man"—here Patrick both turned the crank and blew a retreat on his bugle—"he fought the French with General Braddock, witnessing that man's defeat and death on the banks of the Monongahela."

A river scene rolled slowly into sight, originally intended to represent the Nile. In wonder, the villagers gawked at the painting, unaware that the steep, forested mountains in the background had once been pyramids.

"In his twenty-sixth year he chose to marry," Mr. Fyfe declared, hinting that his subject might better have forgone this folly. "And devoted himself to tending his lands."

The panorama's rollers creaked. A wedding scene appeared, bringing smiles to the crowd—with the exception of Mr. Clapshaw, who'd seen Washington in person, knew he wasn't so plump, and offered his opinion of the painting with a loud snort.

"However," proclaimed Mr. Fyfe, "the hand of Destiny would soon lead him from his tobacco fields to the fields of war."

The wedding, formerly described as that of Ferdinand and Isabella, whose faces had since been repainted, gave way to a distant view of warfare, formerly described as the Battle of Hastings.

"In 1775 he was given command of the Continental

107

army." Mr. Fyfe gestured grandly toward the canvas, wincing at a pain in his bullet-bearing shoulder. "Just a few days before the British, as illustrated here, were met at Bunker Hill." The limner rubbed his shoulder, privately cursing his subject. "And were felled by the score."

Spellbound, Delia marveled at the scene, while Patrick produced an accompaniment of mock gunfire on his drum.

"Looks almighty flat for Bunker Hill," Mr. Clapshaw, who'd fought there, murmured aloud. Mr. Fyfe eyed the man, as did Mrs. Pickett, who recognized him at once and dismissed his paltry objection with a sneer.

The limner continued, narrating Washington's crossing of the Delaware, which river Mr. Clapshaw publicly declared had no such castles along its banks. He recounted the winter at Valley Forge, during which Patrick shook a box containing peas to simulate the sound of hail; followed him through defeat at Monmouth, the final victory at Yorktown, two terms' service as President, and finally arrived at the man's last illness. Through tears, the audience viewed Mr. Fyfe's depiction of Washington's funeral, a scene he'd had to paint from scratch, the pleasing subject of which had made the limner's task seem light. On his drum, Patrick imitated the rifles fired in salute to the leader. Mr. Fyfe then declared that the statesman's life and their canvas had both come to an end. At that, the crowd began to disperse but was instantly halted by Mr. Clapshaw, who, appalled by the profanation of the worship of Washington he'd observed, capped his crescendo of complaints with the announcement that *he* would display his far more faithful waxwork of the fallen President, and relate his lengthy friendship with him, at his wagon—that very afternoon.

III

At one o'clock the church bell clanged and picnic dinners were spread out on the green. Rev. Hooke stood up and blessed the meal, keeping it out of his listeners' mouths while he developed an intricate metaphor in which the soul was represented by a rhubarb pie, the church by the table on which it was cooling, and Satan by the dog standing nearby, hungrily sniffing the air.

Mrs. Pickett sniffed the air as well and watched the villagers commence to eat. She'd brought no food and hadn't been asked to join anyone else's group. Crossing the green, her stomach rumbling, she passed Patrick and his father dining with the Meeses, and scowled to see that even Mr. Clapshaw had been invited to eat with the Beales. Livid, she strode down the road to the Plowshare. She unhitched her horse and climbed into her seat. Then she cracked her whip fiercely, sent her mare into motion—and suddenly saw the beast break free, felt her two-wheeled shay's shafts drop to the ground, and flew forward like a boulder rolling down a mountain, landing in a heap in the road.

She scrambled to her feet and looked around. No one appeared to have seen her, excepting a mosquito whining mockingly in her ear, which witness she quickly slapped out of existence. Seething, she viewed her new calico dress—covered with dirt and torn at the knee—fetched her horse, and studied the dangling straps. The cuts were clean, not ragged as they would have been if the leather had worn out. At once she realized that a knife had been used. A knife in the hand of the wax-work exhibitor—who'd repaid her for not yielding to him on the road.

Her jaw set like a vise, she knotted the ends of the straps and reattached her horse. Then she hitched the mare to a post and marched a circuitous route toward Mr. Clapshaw's wagon. Pausing, she sighted him eating at the opposite end of the green, and smiled. Let the toplofty, twistical scoundrel gorge himself all afternoon if he liked!

She reached his wagon, glanced about, found no padlock on the back door, and climbed in. A few minutes later she slipped back out and made her way back the way she'd come, grinning to glimpse Mr. Clapshaw among the others. Crooked as a dog's hind leg, he was! But being a stranger, she reminded herself, the poor fool hadn't known he was dealing with a Pickett. She stepped into her shay and shook the reins. He'll find out, she thought, and set off for home just as Patrick headed back toward his cart.

He climbed up. In the course of the meal his father had declared they'd be leaving within the hour. In preparation, Patrick counted the coins he'd collected from their audience and stowed his drum and bugle in a trunk. Then he transferred the crank from one roller to the other and began rewinding the panorama.

"Stop!" cried a voice.

Patrick straightened up. He poked his head around the canvas and found Delia Meese staring up at him.

"Roll it back—just a bit. To the right."

Baffled, Patrick did as she asked.

"Perfect," she called out. In rapture, Delia gazed at the canvas. "What a spell the scene casts!"

Patrick peered around the roller and saw that she'd stopped him at their painting of the palace and gardens at Versailles, revised so as to pass for Mt. Vernon.

"The trees—so real you feel you can hear the leaves whispering in the breeze."

Patrick restrained the urge to laugh. She was just like the rest—enthralled by illusion, uninterested in the underlying truth.

"And the hedges. So—sublime."

Patrick stepped down and joined her in front of the panorama.

"You can practically smell the flowers," she went on.

He turned his knowing eyes upon her, marveling at her gullible nature. Then he felt a twinge of guilt for practicing deceit on such a trusting soul—whose family, after all, had fed and lodged him.

"It's just paint."

Delia turned. "Beg pardon?"

Patrick stared at the scene. "It's just paint. Ground up and smeared on a scrap of canvas."

Delia smiled, ignoring the remark. "And such a wonderful feeling of depth. As if those tiny hills in the background were truly a three-days' ride away."

"Nothing but the laws of perspective," offered Patrick.

To their right, the crowd was following Mr. Clapshaw in the direction of his wagon.

"And the *richness* of the green!" gushed Delia.

"Prussian blue mixed with yellow," Patrick explained.

Impervious to his comments, Delia approached the canvas more closely. "Judging by the angle of light, it looks like early afternoon."

Curiously, Patrick stepped forward, never having noticed this detail.

"I see that there aren't any birds about—no doubt they're hiding from the heat of the sun. It would seem, then, that the weather is warm. And looking at the leaves, close to midsummer. July, I'd say." She faced Patrick. "Am I right?"

Dumbfounded by such involvement in a painting he'd never given a second thought to, Patrick, dazed, nodded his head and found himself gazing at it with fresh interest.

"You can imagine the heavenly scent of the gardens drifting through the house," Delia continued. "With the windows open the way they are."

Far off, Mr. Clapshaw could be heard describing his long association with General Washington.

"And, it being July, you know the air's heavy. Looks like a storm might be building to the left."

113

Mesmerized, Patrick studied the painting, his face cooled by a breeze that rippled the canvas and seemed to bring the landscape to life.

"If you come closer," said Delia, "and throw back your head, the scene blends right in with the trees overhead."

Patrick stepped forward. He arched his spine and, like a magician fooling himself with his tricks, found pleasure in the illusion that the world of the canvas extended all around him.

"One seamless sky seems to stretch over all," murmured Delia, entranced by the thought. Then she reminded herself sharply that Patrick was leaving shortly.

"You can almost imagine we're standing in the garden, alone," she spoke up.

Patrick nodded, Mr. Clapshaw's voice fading in his ears.

"That we're not in Vermont, but at a palace—in Persia."

Head tilted, Patrick slowly became aware of Delia's hand slipping into his.

"And that you're a young prince, on a journey," she continued. "And that I'm the princess you've come to claim."

Knowing she'd little time to impress her image indelibly into his mind, she glanced quickly about, found no one in sight, and planted a kiss on Patrick's cheek—at which moment a cry went up from the crowd.

The pair parted at once, dashed around the cart, and stared at the waxwork exhibitor's wagon—where Mr. Clapshaw had described Washington's manners, his taste in reading and choice in clothes, collected ten cents from each member of the audience, and at last thrown open the wagon door: revealing the figure of the nation's first President with a noose around his neck, hanging from the ceiling.

Dumbstruck, Mr. Clapshaw gaped at the waxwork. Then he leapt inside, cut the rope, and, bearing Washington to his chair, set him down and threw off the noose. Desperately, he inspected the model, found it appeared to be unharmed—and suddenly realized who was to blame. Whirling about, he shot out of the wagon, sliced a path through the center of the crowd, and stormed across the village green.

Patrick watched the man striding his way and wondered what had happened. His father, who'd refused to pay the man's charge and had walked toward the Meeses' to retrieve his horse, turned around and viewed Mr. Clapshaw, trailed by the throng, with similar interest—then saw that the man was headed for his cart.

Mr. Clapshaw eyed Patrick, emitted a snort, and climbed up onto the bed of the cart.

"Didn't care for my remarks on your show, I see!" To the amazement of the gathering below, he then took the top of the canvas in his hands and ripped the scene of Mt. Vernon in half.

"*There's* for your monstrous, sly-dog trickery!" he yelled triumphantly at Patrick. Then he spotted Mr. Fyfe running toward the cart, snatched up Mrs. Meese's black cherry brandy, pulled the cork, and poured the contents over the tops of the rollers.

"The man's mad!" Patrick shouted out.

Seeing the boy's innocent look, several villagers joined in restraining Mr. Clapshaw just as Mr. Fyfe arrived. Astounded by the man's unwarranted attack, the limner inspected the damage, found the panorama had been stained black, and set off toward Mr. Clapshaw's wagon. The crowd, unsure with whom to side, followed curiously behind, saw him open his knife and climb in, and looked on with mingled horror and glee as Washington's arm, still clothed in its coat, came flying out the wagon door. Followed quickly by another arm. Then a left leg. Then a right. Then Mr. Fyfe himself, who jumped to the ground holding Washington's head, reared back and heaved it with all his might, watching it sail high through the air, then hurtle to earth like a meteor and explode into chips beside the cannon.

116

"*That's* the treatment *you* deserve!" he roared in Mr. Clapshaw's direction. Climbing back in the wagon, he commenced breaking the furniture, and was shortly stopped by a trio of men. Arms flailing, the two itinerants were returned to their respective corners of the green, snarling like dogs at each other when they passed, and were instructed to do no further damage to the already gravely wounded public peace.

In disbelief, Mr. Clapshaw stared at the wax limbs strewn about the green. One at a time he bore them into his wagon, as if removing the dead from a battlefield. The splinters of wax that had been Washington's head he reverently placed in his cooking pot. Sick at heart, he shuffled back to his wagon, chagrined that such a thing should happen on the Fourth of July, in the very nation Washington had fought to found.

He unhitched his team and climbed up to his seat. Numbly, he placed the cooking pot at his side. He wondered what he'd do now—then vowed to melt down the disassembled wax limbs and reshape them into a new Washington. Never would he give up his post as the first President's footman! Shaking his reins, he set off toward the crossroads, arrived there just ahead of the limners, and delivered his opinion that attacking the waxwork of a President might possibly be a capital

117

crime. He then expressed his fond wish to see them again, preferably dangling from the gallows, and turned his horse and wagon to the south.

Mr. Fyfe laughed bitterly. "Buffle-brained fool!" He flicked his reins and headed to the north. "That's what becomes of a man when he's the dupe of sham, every mite and morsel." He glanced at Patrick. "The *real* crime is showing his fool waxwork to the public, spreading the worship of worthless heroes."

Mr. Fyfe paused and blotted his brow. "Which we've been guilty of as well. But no more!" He smiled, filled with a sense of decision. "I tell you, this episode was the best thing that ever happened to us! I'm positively glad that panorama's ruined!"

Patrick emerged from his reverie and studied his father a moment.

"Yes indeed! No more deceiving people! We'll burn that canvas. And our brushes, too. And take up a more respectable trade. Giving lectures on the *real* Washington perhaps! Traveling about, helping people to see the world as it truly is!"

Inflamed by the notion of striking out against illusion in all its many forms, Mr. Fyfe feverishly poured forth his plans. All of which was scarcely heard by Patrick, who, though he'd long been instructed that love was the most dangerous of all deceptions, discovered himself recalling with pleasure the feeling of Delia's lips on his cheek. And despite his father's determination to free the innumerable slaves of sham, he himself, basking in the memory of that rapturous moment, found himself viewing the countryside and imagining it to be not Vermont but Persia, and himself a prince.

Country Pay

JONATHAN PAUSED on the porch, eyes alert.

He glanced to his right. Then to his left. Warily he descended the steps.

In one hand he carried a pewter lantern. In the other he held a mug of cider. In his head he bore the welcome notion that the whole episode was surely a dream.

He crept down the walk. The sun had set, its train of light lingering in the west. He looked back at the house, saw one window was lit, then turned down the path that led to the creek. The air was chill, the ground layered with leaves. Like an eye loose in its socket, his lantern beam picked out a milkweed stalk, then his shoe top, then a bird's nest, exposed and empty, in a tree.

He reached the bridge that crossed the creek. Cautiously he stepped onto it, crouched, and set down the lantern, as instructed. Beside it he placed the mug of cider. Sitting, he glimpsed the shimmer of water in the pair of pools on the other side of the creek. He made out the cypress tree beside one and the poplar planted beside the other. He studied the apple orchard behind them. And he wondered how he, Jonathan Wardwell, a peddler of dyes and essences, had come to be in this condition—sitting on a bridge, shivering in the cold, awaiting a visit from the spirits of Mr. and Mrs. Nathaniel Tewkes.

The meetinghouse bell was chiming noon when he'd ambled into New Canaan. It was the first day of November, Jonathan's birthday. Overhead, a flock of geese was flying south. Jonathan heard their honking, glanced up, and was reminded again that time was running out. In three weeks he'd be trudging back into Boston. Disgraced—unless he executed a miracle of salesmanship and got rid of *it* here, or somewhere in between. Small chance! the peddler mocked himself. Then he remembered that he was seventeen now, a full year older than he'd been the day before. Straightening the narrow, coffinlike tin trunk he carried upon one shoulder, he endeavored to adopt a confident gait, sprang up a set of steps to his left, and resolutely strode into the Plowshare.

"Good day to you, ma'am—and a fine day at that!" He brushed a clump of red hair from his eyes. "Might you be needing a pound of wooden nutmegs? A pint of well water bottled as perfume? A clock guaranteed to grind to a halt the moment I'm half a mile away?"

Jonathan grinned good-naturedly. His father, founder of Wardwell and Sons, Merchants of Herbs, Dyestuffs, and Extracts, a man who'd begun as a trunk peddler

124

himself, had assured him this ploy would win the favor of ninty-nine customers out of one hundred.

"Not interested," Mrs. Beale snapped, returning to stuffing a mattress with cornhusks.

Jonathan felt his smile expire and knew that he'd found the one resister.

"In truth," he stammered, "I'm selling dyes. Gathered from every corner of the globe." He set down his trunk and pried off the lid. "Indigo, to transform the dirtiest sheep's wool from gray to brilliant blue. Fustic for yellow. Logwood for black. Spanish cochineal. Madder from France." The peddler raised his eyes from his stock. "The firm of Wardwell and Sons, which I serve, has built its success upon one simple motto: 'Give the people what they need.' " Jonathan resurrected his smile.

"Don't need any dyes," Mrs. Beale declared.

Frantically, Jonathan rummaged through his trunk, as if for an answer to the woman's reply.

"Perhaps then you're short on essences. Sweet-smelling oil of bergamot. Peppermint extract. Essence of wintergreen—known to be wondrous at reviving sore muscles."

Mrs. Beale shook her head, tossed a log on the fire behind her, and commenced sewing up her mattress.

"Naturally," Jonathan sputtered, "I also have various goods taken in trade." Goods, his father had made clear to him, which a peddler must strive to sell or trade at a profit farther along his route. "A beaver pelt. Two pounds of dried peas. A pair of spectacles, hardly used." He patted the bulging left pocket of his coat. "Plus nails." He shook his right pocket. "And bullets."

Mrs. Beale stepped forward, picked through his trunk, and emerged with a rusty padlock in her hand.

"Might you be selling the key that goes with it?"

Astonished at the prospect of a sale, Jonathan desperately pawed through his stock. "Yes, ma'am! If I can just put my fingers on it. . . ." Hadn't his father exhorted him to keep his trunk neat and well organized? Cursing his born inclination toward chaos, he lifted a bag leaking peas and found it.

Mrs. Beale smiled, took the key from him, then suddenly stared at the peddler in fear. "You weren't thinking of trading this thief-stopper for your lodging, I trust."

"No, ma'am!" he replied, assuming she meant the remark to convey her calculation of the padlock's worth. "Twenty cents is all I'm asking." Then he recalled that he'd traded thirty cents' worth of madder for it three towns back and fumed at his howling stupidity.

Mrs. Beale mused on his offer, inserted the key— and found it wouldn't turn. "Reckon *any* price is too much for this." She handed it back. "Rusted shut."

Chastising himself for ever having accepted it in trade

in the first place, Jonathan labored feverishly with the key, blushed, gave up, berated himself, then plucked a small book from his trunk and placed it, in lieu of the lock, in Mrs. Beale's hand.

"There, on the contrary, is an object guaranteed to give full satisfaction." This, he knew, was a monstrous lie. He also knew that unless he managed to sell it his entire future was blighted. "A book from which all will reap pleasure and wonder."

Mrs. Beale opened its black leather cover. Her features twitched. Her eyes narrowed. "What in creation is it?" she demanded.

"The Bible, ma'am," Jonathan replied.

The woman's eyebrows shot up in dismay.

"Put in the Chinese tongue," he added, pointing to the name, at the bottom of the page, of the missionary society that had printed it, twelve of whose copies had inexplicably turned up in a crate of East Indian indigo.

Mrs. Beale eyed the book with suspicion. "Looks more like the Devil's work to me. And what would I want with it even if it weren't?"

This was a question Jonathan had foreseen the morning his father had handed him the book. The same morning in May on which he'd been told that, as with his four elder brothers, his joining the firm of Wardwell and Sons was not a hereditary right but rather a privilege, to be granted upon display of Mercantile Ability. Which quality would be deemed present if he returned, as had his brothers before him, with the Bible no longer in his trunk.

"Folks find all manner of uses for 'em." Jonathan studied Mrs. Beale's features. "Why, I reckon I've sold a dozen at least. Including one just yesterday noon to the deacon's wife over in Hubbardsville."

He searched for signs of this falsehood's impact.

"No, thank you," Mrs. Beale barked and thrust the book into Jonathan's hands.

"They say that it doesn't take any bushel of brains to learn to cipher it out." The peddler smiled hopefully. "And that once a person gets used to it, it takes ten men and a mule to drag 'em away from it and back to the English."

Mrs. Beale snorted and returned to her chair.

"I don't usually take less than a dollar for 'em." Jonathan gazed at the fire, then at the mattress Mrs. Beale was stitching, then recalled his attempts to sleep the night before on the stony ground, in the rain. "But not being the sort to think about profit when it comes to an item such as this, I'll consider a bed for the night as full payment."

The woman's eyes opened in alarm.

128

"Naturally," he added quickly, "I could make myself handy with an ax, splitting wood."

Mrs. Beale threw down her mattress and stood up. "Get out with you—now! And don't come back!"

Jonathan hastily packed his trunk.

"I wouldn't give you so much as a bedbug for your confounded book of chicken scratchings! And I'll not take in any sellers of dyes—or any other of you widow-swindling, lie-peddling coming-and-going men!"

Coat pockets jangling, Jonathan dashed out the door, which slammed with finality behind him. Mystified by the woman's outburst, he lifted his trunk to his shoulder and set off, passing the village green and its row of towering maples—now naked as wrestlers, poised to grapple with the winter wind.

He stopped at the next three houses he came to. Recalling his father's advice to let his customers talk so that he might learn how best to induce them to purchase something, Jonathan suffered through two family histories, plus Rev. Hooke's hour-long discourse on a pair of scissors, bought from a peddler, that refused to cut anything whatsoever—without being rewarded with a single sale. Continuing on, he followed his father's counsel in learning the state of local opinion concerning the coming election. Putting this knowledge to use, the peddler hazarded a comment on the contest and at once lost a sale of indigo to a man who, unlike most of his neighbors, favored Jefferson over President Adams.

He left the village, passed by a house with a jack-o'-lantern perched on its porch, but felt too disgusted with himself to knock.

How could he be such a failure at peddling? His brothers had sold out their stock *and* their plaguey Chinese Bibles in a month or two. In triumph, they'd been welcomed home by their father, who'd taken the white shirt each had worn, washed it, dyed it royal purple, and lowered it over the head of the new member of Wardwell and Sons the following morning. Jonathan fingered his own filthy collar. Would he, the youngest, be the only son denied this solemn investiture?

Shifting his trunk from one shoulder to the other, he studied his shadow, resembling that of a pallbearer endlessly searching for the graveyard. His brothers had borne the same trunk, filled with the same merchandise. What was their secret? Suddenly it occurred to him that their knack might lie in being *true* Wardwells, born with commerce in their blood and bones—while he, Jonathan speculated, might perhaps have been adopted instead.

The peddler stopped in the middle of the road. Wasn't his own hair red, and theirs blond? Weren't they all taller than he, and quicker-witted, racing through their sums at school while he struggled along, far behind?

He pushed on, hearing geese overhead. Then again, he reasoned, the only difference between them might be that they had given their Bibles away, or buried them, or tossed them into the Charles River. Cheered by this conjectured deceit, Jonathan viewed a stream to his left—then chased the notion out of his head. Never would he stoop to such fraud! He *could* sell that unreadable book, and he *would*—and prove to the world that he was a Wardwell!

Looking up at the geese, anxious to gain membership in his own flock, he knocked at a house and sold two cakes of indigo. Soon after, he met a man on the road and traded four ounces of wintergreen oil for a button from General Washington's coat. Pondering this transaction with pride, knowing he'd gotten the best of the man, he trudged up a hill, spotted a house at the top, marched down the path leading to it—then stopped.

The house was like no other he'd ever seen. It was white, so blindingly bright in the sun that it seemed to radiate light like a star. A flight of steps led up to a porch, upon which stood four massive columns supporting a giant portico. Jonathan thought back to a drawing of the Parthenon he'd once seen in a book. To his right, he saw that the land sloped down toward a creek, spanned by a strange-looking bridge. Beyond it he spied a pair of pools, glinting in the afternoon sun and hypnotically engaging his gaze.

Curiously, the peddler walked on. He approached the steps to the house, started up—and was startled to find himself progressively viewing the kerchief, then the face, then the shawl, then the shoes of a young woman, lost in thought, in a rocker.

"Good day," Jonathan fumbled. "Ma'am." He wondered why he'd not glimpsed her from afar, then saw she was dressed, like the house, all in white. "And a sightly day at that!" he added.

His customer gave no sign of agreeing. Ensconced in her chair, her sole symptoms of life were her eyes' patient inspection of the peddler and her fingers' absent toying with the tip of one strand of her molasses-brown hair.

"Wooden nutmegs—twelve for a dollar!"

Jonathan smiled heartily. He studied the woman's pale face, long and narrow as a weaver's shuttle, and was struck by the oddity that she wasn't husking corn or slicing apples as his other buyers had been.

"Pins made of tin—guaranteed to bend!"

The woman stared at him soberly.

132

"A clock . . ." The peddler felt his smile collapsing. "Actually, ma'am, it's dyes I'm selling."

Jonathan put down his trunk, lifted the lid off, and propped up his grin. "The tools of miraculous transformation—changing plain white into royal purple, drab gray into emerald green. 'Give the people what they need' has ever been the motto of Wardwell and Sons. Might you be lacking cochineal? Indigo? Oak bark? Madder or peach leaves?"

"I shan't be needing any," she answered softly. "Thank you just the same."

"But what about essences? Oil of peppermint. Bergamot. Wintergreen. Bottled cologne water."

"I'll have no use for them, I assure you."

Jonathan puzzled over her replies. He placed his hand on the Chinese Bible, then decided to first follow his father's advice and draw his buyer out.

"That wintergreen's wondrous at curing a cough." Jonathan rose and looked about him. "But not half as wondrous as this house of yours."

The woman smiled faintly.

"Never laid eyes on one like it before." Jonathan studied one of the columns.

"My father had great respect for the ancients," his customer stated, viewing the column.

"That's plain," said the peddler.

"Especially the Greeks." She seemed to brighten at the thought of the man. "He named me Ida after the mountain said to be near Troy," she volunteered. She turned her eyes toward a hill to the east. "When he moved us here, when I was an infant, he named that rise on our land Mount Olympus."

Jonathan eyed the hilltop, wondering how he was supposed to put this information to use in selling the Bible.

"Might your mother be about?" he asked. "I've an item I'm certain she'll want to see."

"My mother's been dead a crow's age," Ida answered.

Jonathan privately cursed himself. Hadn't his father warned him not to touch on subjects unpleasant to his buyers?

"My father buried her beyond the creek. Then he built Tartarus around her."

Jonathan cocked his head. "Tartarus?"

"The Greek kingdom of the dead."

Ida rose, revealing herself taller than the peddler. "He named the creek the River Styx. In place of Charon, the ferryman who was said to row the souls across, he built a bridge made to look like a boat."

Jonathan struggled to hide his amazement.

"He cleared the ground on the other side—the Asphodel Fields, where the ghosts hunt deer. Beyond, around my mother's grave, he planted the land in apple trees to signify the Elysian Fields—a land of fruit and perpetual joy.''

Jonathan, shocked to hear of someone who didn't believe in Heaven and Hell, was simultaneously thrilled at the prospect of having at last found a buyer for his book.

He cleared his throat. ''Would your father be at home?''

''Home in his Elysian Fields,'' answered Ida. ''He took a fever, this past July.''

Jonathan swore at himself for having asked. ''I'm almighty sorry to hear that, ma'am.''

''Miss,'' she corrected him.

Jonathan blushed, wondering if he'd left any blunders uncommitted. ''Perhaps then, miss, in your time of grief, and being so very broadminded as you are, you might care to comfort yourself with this.'' He pulled out the Bible and handed it to her. ''One of the great holy books of the East. Printed in the original tongue—to avoid the raft of errors that always creep into any translation,'' he explained.

Ida sat down and opened the volume.

''I don't mind saying I'm eager to sell.''

Anxiously, he watched Ida flip through it.

''I'll take country pay in place of money—goose feathers, tallow, ashes, spun wool. . . .''

The peddler willed her not to close the book, an order she disobeyed at once.

"I'll take anything for it!" he pleaded with her. "Something you'd just as soon be rid of!"

Ida smiled politely. "I've really no use for it. Thank you all the same."

Imagining his father's eyes upon him, Jonathan picked through his trunk, determined not to leave without making a sale.

"Of course, I've got all manner of trade goods." He displayed a tinder wheel on his palm, gazing down upon it proudly. "First cousin to brand-new. Guaranteed to send out a shower of sparks and get your tinder lit before you can blink."

The peddler looked up—and was astonished to find his customer's features frozen in place, her eyes locked on the tinder wheel.

"Twenty-five cents will buy it," he spoke up.

Her iced eyes came alive. "I've no need for it, thank you."

"I've also got dried peas," he announced. "As well as a beaver pelt, nails, lead bullets. A fine pair of spectacles, hardly used. . . ."

Instantly, Jonathan regretted the words. Spectacles were for the old, not the young.

"Naturally," he stammered, castigating himself, "to

136

be saved—for the future.'' Marveling at his thickheaded-
ness, he quickly tucked them back in the trunk.

"There won't be any future for me,'' Ida declared
matter-of-factly.

Jonathan stopped his rummaging. Bewildered, he
stared at the woman.

"Perhaps,'' she continued, "if you're heading south,
you'd leave a letter concerning the matter at the Seven
Swans, in Billingston.''

Uncertainly, Jonathan nodded his head and followed
Ida inside the house. The front room was vast and richly
furnished. Glancing about, he felt watched by the subjects of the paintings and busts displayed about him:
Zeus, Athena, Socrates, a centaur, and sundry other gods
and mortals.

Ida handed the peddler a letter. "My uncle will no
doubt lift his eyebrows to find himself the possessor of
all this.''

Jonathan glanced at the hearth, noting the absence
of sliced apples and pumpkins strung above it, drying
for winter.

"And why is it,'' he ventured, "that you won't be
here?''

Ida added a pair of logs to the fire. "Because I've
only three days left to live.''

Jonathan viewed her in disbelief. "You look everlast-

137

ing healthy to me." Could she have some invisible ailment, he wondered—something for which wintergreen oil was prescribed?

"My mother looked healthy as well, I'm sure. Till a spark, from this hearth, lit on her dress." She crouched and studied the blaze before her. "It was called an accident. But then, a year later, I heard a man tell my father of a girl who'd drowned herself in a well, just as her own mother had done. That was the same day I'd gone to the pool."

"The pool?"

"Across the bridge, in Tartarus. The one that's marked by the cypress tree is the Pool of Forgetfulness. Most souls were said to drink there at once, divesting themselves of their former lives. The one by the poplar is the Pool of Memory, conferring the power of prophecy."

Jonathan recalled seeing them and began to wish he'd passed the house by.

"I was forbidden to cross the bridge, but I was just four, and didn't know any better. It was hot. I splashed in the Pool of Memory, and got a drop of the water in my mouth. That night I dreamed, and was shown the future. Three old women stood above me and explained that my mother had taken her own life—by jabbing the burning logs with the poker till a spark jumped

138

onto her sleeve. Then they said I was destined to follow her—and would die at exactly her age, the same way."

The peddler saw that she was eyeing the black, barb-tipped poker leaning against the bricks.

"And you believed them?" Jonathan asked.

"There's no point trying to escape your fate. As the Greeks, and my father, to your left, said often."

The peddler turned and peered at the painting of a long-legged man wrapped in a toga, identified at the bottom as being Mr. Nathaniel Tewkes.

"He himself sensed he wasn't destined to live long. He engaged two limners to paint that portrait—the only likeness of him—this summer. Exactly five days before he died."

"But you simply had a dream," the peddler protested.

Ida stood up and approached the painting hanging beside her father's. "I have my mother's brown hair, you'll agree."

Jonathan gazed up at the portrait, surprised to find Mrs. Tewkes' face round as an orange, in contrast to her daughter's.

"I've her brown eyes as well," Ida added.

The peddler considered this evidence, which she clearly believed confirmed her fate.

"But do you want to end your life?" he asked.

Ida drifted back toward the hearth. "The madness apparently comes on one swiftly." She pulled up a chair and faced the flames, seeming to address them rather than Jonathan.

"November fourth is three days away. On that day I'll be twenty-two years, four months, and five days. Just as my mother was. I've no doubt I'll desire to follow her then."

She reached out and took the poker in her hand. Gazing serenely at the blaze, as if at the familiar face of a friend, she tentatively prodded a log.

"There's no law about it," Jonathan pleaded. "I don't reckon what I ate for breakfast was exactly what my father ate the morning of *his* seventeenth birthday. There's absolutely—"

"It's your birthday?" Ida demanded, suddenly whirling about.

"Yes, ma'am. Miss, that is," Jonathan answered.

Ida rushed across the room toward him. "Then you'll stay the night, and speak to them—won't you?"

The peddler stared at her. "Speak to who?"

"To my parents, of course. They'll be coming—I know it!"

"But they're dead!"

"And this is All Souls' Eve. The one night in the

140

year when the dead can leave the underworld. Though the only ones able to see and address them are those who were born on this day—like yourself."

Jonathan gaped at Ida, unaware he was the possessor of this power.

"My father always said they were released at sunset. And that those who would speak to them carried a lantern, in order to guide the spirits to them."

"But I've never once seen a spirit!" the peddler exclaimed.

"No doubt you haven't happened to be near any."

Jonathan pondered this answer, glanced outside, and saw that the sun was low. He knew he needed a place to stay—unless, he reminded himself, he wanted to shiver on the ground, as he had the night before. He faced the fire, realizing that there might not be another house for miles.

"I remember my father saying that the spirits long for their favorite food or drink." Ida looked out at a stand of trees. "I could give you some cider, from the Greening apples. My father loved them best of all— said their juice was the equal of the nectar of the gods."

Jonathan found himself gazing at Tartarus.

"You'll have a feather mattress to sleep on. And Indian pudding and apple pie for supper."

141

Deciding at once that he didn't actually believe in spirits anyway, and that, therefore, he'd be a fool to refuse, Jonathan set Ida's letter on the mantel and brought his trunk inside the house.

"What is it you want me to ask them?" he inquired, privately making light of the question.

Ida turned toward her parents' portraits. "Ask them what the afterlife is like. Assure them that I miss them both." She cast a long glance at the fire. "And tell them I'll be joining them soon."

A breeze blew over Jonathan. The few leaves on the trees shivered, as if feverish. Huddling against the rounded, boatlike sides of the bridge, he looked down it, toward Tartarus.

His father had always scoffed at ghost talk. No one else he knew had ever met one. In his seventeen years, Jonathan, who was said to be able to see them, hadn't caught a glimpse. With the sun departed and the sky now black, he found himself clinging to these arguments.

On the other hand, he told himself, if spirits indeed wandered the earth, he'd have nothing to fear from those of Ida's parents. They hadn't any score to settle with him. They were probably the most refined haunts you could find. And if they *did* come, and report that life in the Elysian Fields was almighty mournful, it might change Ida's mind about joining them. Something he felt sure she'd otherwise do.

For her sake, Jonathan decided to wait a full hour for his guests. Three hours later he was still at his post, ruminating upon their daughter.

How in the world could she be so sure that her mother had meant to end her own life? It certainly seemed an improbable method. What seemed far more likely was that Ida had simply been scared to the marrow by the tale of the girl who'd drowned in the well just like her mother. Thinking back to the portrait, he'd have never guessed it was Ida's mother. They scarcely looked related—yet Ida saw only the few similarities.

Jonathan listened to the creek beneath him and noticed Orion half risen in the east. He mused on his miserable record as a peddler and wondered again whether he might in fact not be his father's son—fated, unlike Ida, not to follow his steps, but to take a different path.

He waited the better part of another hour, cursing Ida and the cold. If she weren't so fool-headed, he reflected, he'd be sleeping on a feather mattress at that moment. Was he really expecting her parents' souls to come strolling across the bridge? he asked himself. What if they *liked* the afterlife? He turned to see if Ida's light was out and discovered that the house was hidden by the slope. Seeing that his own light was low, he picked up the lantern, studied the candle, vowed he'd wait only another half inch's worth—then heard what sounded like a footfall on the bridge.

Jonathan froze. His senses opened wide, till he felt he could hear a leaf drop a mile off. Turning slowly to his right, he held out the lantern but found its light died before it reached the end of the bridge.

No doubt, he reasoned, it was an acorn falling. Then he heard another footstep on the wood. His hand, the lantern, and its beam trembled. Peering fearfully into the blackness, he made out the sound of another pair of feet, heard breathing—and suddenly spied two eyes.

Leaping up in fright, he knocked over the cider—and glimpsed the huge outline of a bear nosing toward him. Petrified, unsolaced by the visit of this guest in place of the ghosts he'd expected, he quickly decided his vigil was over, snatched up the mug, and dashed back to the house.

He opened the door and found Ida by the fire.

"You're back!" She smiled, sprang up from her chair, and took the empty mug from his hand. "They drank every drop of the cider, I see."

The peddler, still recovering from his fright and unsure what to say, smiled feebly.

"Did you mention it came from the Greening apples?"

Reluctant to challenge her firm faith in spirits, Jonathan nodded and eyed the staircase, wishing he could simply slip out of the room.

"And what did they say about the life beyond?"

He avoided Ida's gaze, fixed on his eyes. Turning, he warmed his hands at the fire, searched his wits for something to say—and decided to apply the Wardwell and Sons motto.

"They said it's everlasting cold."

"Cold?" Ida's voice was sharp with surprise.

"That's what they said. And damp as well."

Ida crossed the room toward her parents' portraits, studying them with concern.

"They said time slogs along dreadful slow."

Ida appeared dismayed by this news.

"You told them I miss them both dearly?" she asked.

"Yes, miss."

"And that I'll be joining them soon?"

"I told them." Jonathan paused. "But they said that your time is a long way off," he added, amazed to hear the words leaving his mouth.

Ida's eyes widened. "But how can that be? November fourth is three days away."

Frantically, Jonathan hunted a reply. "They said you weren't really their child," he declared, having no idea where the words had come from. "They said a woman passing through town had died in childbirth—and her

145

husband from smallpox." The peddler was as shocked by this announcement as Ida. "So they took you in. Before they came here."

Ida's face became as stiff as a mask. "Back when they lived in England?" she murmured.

"That's right—in England!" Jonathan turned. His hands, clasped behind him, fluttered nervously. "Your mother said that on account of her accident she never had a chance to tell you. Your father said he meant to, but never did. For fear you might think that they didn't love you." Jonathan licked his lips and prayed her parents would forgive him. "Which they did—and still do. Just the same as they would their own."

Ida seated herself in a chair. All of a sudden her blank gaze became focused.

"Did they say," she asked, leaning toward Jonathan, "what age the woman was when she died?"

"Barely sixteen!" he replied with conviction, disqualifying her dreamed prophecy.

Ida sat silently in her chair.

Worried that he might have turned her against her parents, Jonathan gnawed on his tongue. Then he watched her rise and approach their portraits, and looked on with relief as she pulled out a handkerchief and lovingly wiped the dust from the frames.

146

"I reckon I'll put that feather mattress you mentioned to use," the peddler spoke up.

Ida, absorbed by her task, didn't turn. "Upstairs and to your right," she absently replied.

Jonathan gave his hands a last warming and started gratefully up the stairs.

When, eight hours later, he descended, the sun was just sprouting up from the hills. He saw that Ida's letter was no longer on the mantel, but hadn't yet heard the sound of her steps. Approaching his trunk, he was pleased to discover half an apple pie sitting atop it.

Hungrily, Jonathan devoured it, wondering how far he'd get that day, hoping he'd have more success with his selling. Then he hoisted his trunk up to his shoulder, tiptoed out, set off down the path—and spotted her across the creek, bending over the pool by the cypress, the Pool of Forgetfulness, cupping the water up to her mouth. Freeing herself once and for all, the peddler hoped, from her delusion of doom.

Marching ahead, he reached the road, and struck out southward toward Billingston. It wasn't until he'd walked four miles, made his way down a path toward a house, and opened his trunk for a farmer's wife that he found she'd traded her poker for his Bible.